COMMON CRIMINALS

— L. A. Crime Stories —

Larry Fondation

Paradise / Asylum Arts / 2002

Acknowledgments

Grateful acknowledgment is made to the following publications, where some of the stories in this collection were previously published:

"Driving Cars," *Asylum;* "Deportation at Breakfast," *Asylum* and numerous anthologies, including *Flash Fiction* (WW Norton) and *Something to Declare* (Oxford); "Cuckold," "Cuckold II," "Animal Rights," and "Make-up," *Fiction International;* "Civil Unrest," *Bakunin;* "Accidents," and "Little Things" (in slightly different form), *Five Fingers Review;* "Stolen Goods," *The Pittsburgh Quarterly.*

ISBN 1-878580-70-1

Library of Congress Catalog Number: 2002106594

Cover art by Sean Newton

Special thanks to my wife, Kathy Hayes, and to my daughters, Lilly, Julie, and Malaika.

For Barry Graham and for Amy Turner
Who both know why

Asylum Arts
5847 Sawmill Road
Paradise, CA 95969

Common Criminals

Contents

"All the hip cats on the corner,
They don't look so sharp no mo,'
`Coz all the good times is over
And the squares don't have no dough."

Jimmy Witherspoon
Skid Row Blues (1947)

"Indeed what goes `round comes `round. The
America we are making for others is ultimately
the America we will make for ourselves. It will
not be on the other side of town. It will be right
outside our front doors."

Mikal Gilmore, "Easy Target: Why Tupac
Should Be Heard Before He's Buried"
Rolling Stone, October 31,1996

Common Criminals

Cuckold

I.

I ask for money from a homeless man.
He gives me fifty cents. Two quarters. I spend them at a peep show.
It is humid just after a rain. The streetlights seem dim.
I don't know where to go next.

II.

A man sprays the pool table with bullets. I know him. He is a regular here at the Brig.

He hits one guy in the leg and he destroys a table, riddling it with small holes.

He sits down at the bar and orders a beer.

No one says a word. A young couple at the next table over resume playing. The woman is beating the man at eight ball.

The man with the gun finishes his beer, shoots out a Budweiser clock, then orders another beer.

Three of the four pool tables are full now again.

The man with the gun is perhaps forty-five. His mother walks into the bar. She sits down next to him and he buys her a drink. She is perhaps sixty-five and she is wearing a black leather miniskirt, a crop top, and open-toed, spike heels. Her hair is bleached blonde and her nails are long and red. Judging by her stomach muscles, you can tell she works out with weights. Men half her age stop to stare. When she sees the gun on the bar, she slaps her son hard across the face. He hands her the gun and buys her another drink, this time a double Jack Daniels.

III.

I want some ass, a nice piece of ass. It's crazy I don't have some ass tonight, just crazy. Instead: cable. I wonder what's on cable. HBO. Home

Beat Off. Shit. I forgot. They shut off my cable. Now I don't have cable. This is crazy. Really crazy.

IV.

I go outside knowing what awaits me. They don't hesitate. One works on my face, the other on my stomach. I decide it's best not to fight back. After ten or twelve blows I fall to the ground. They kick me a few times, then they stop. I wait for the next hits. They do not come. I hear footsteps; they are getting further away. I cannot get up off the pavement, but at least I'm alive.

V.

We spent a lot of time killing bugs. First we tried to do it ourselves. We would stand by the sink, our shoes in our hands, the lights off. She would count to fifty. Then we'd turn on the lights and attack the kitchen counter and the sink. The best we did in one round was 62 cockroaches.

We moved on to store-bought products—sprays, bombs, motels, traps. We tried all kinds of brands: Raid, Combat, Holiday, Black Flag.

Both she and I put several hours each day into this activity. We began to look forward to it. We developed favorites in both brands and product types. I felt employed!

We cultivated and introduced all kinds of bugs into our home: ants, roaches, silverfish. We thought about rats and mice but decided against it.

When at last we decided to end it all, we had to call exterminators. We tried three or four before one finally did the trick. I am not saying which one. I publish a newsletter now on effective removal of pesky insects. I get a dollar a copy. It sells fairly well.

VI.

With a small inheritance I buy a dozen whores, both men and women. I meet them at the Ski Room on Sunset near Bronson. I buy them all drinks, then I take them up to a room in the scuzzy hotel next door. I watch them fuck. When I clap my hands, they change partners.

At the end I pick one out—a short, fat chick—and I do her up the ass.

When it is over I take some pills and drink some beer and fall asleep.

VII.

We were just kids. At Clifton's all-night cafeteria Richie went through the line and stole a piece of apple pie. He sat down at a long formica table. At the other end, a bearded man of about fifty sat before a plate of leftovers. An old woman with enormous tits walked in and I whistled at her. She thought I was making fun of her, but I wasn't.

The fluorescent lights were hurting my eyes. I lit up a joint. It was nearly three AM and we'd been up all night drinking and smoking.

Richie took one bite of the pie and spit it back onto the plate. He went up to the counter and asked to see the manager.

"I want to see the manager," he said.

"Just a minute, young man," the cashier said.

The manager walked over to where Richie was standing. He was a tall, thin man of about thirty in a wrinkled white shirt, a thin, striped tie, and blue corduroy pants. He was going bald.

"Can I help you?" he asked, a bit nasal. Richie hated nasal.

"Yes," Richie said, holding up the plate like it was Holy Communion, then spitting on it again for emphasis. "This pie is stale."

"I'm sorry," said the manager.

Richie shook his head vigorously from side to side. "I am never, ever going to steal a piece of apple pie from this place again."

Richie marched out slowly and in a huff. The manager looked at me.

"Are you with him?" he asked.

Outside I passed Richie the joint.

VIII.

The National Guardsmen are on Hollywood Boulevard.

A group of my friends is breaking windows and I am sitting on the curbstone, jerking off.

She walks over and smiles at me. She asks if she can finish me off.

"Sure," I say.

She sits down beside me.

She has ultra-long nails, filed pointy, and she draws blood when she strokes me.

The cops come by and chase away the people who are breaking windows. They catch one and hit him with a baton; another is running fast and carrying a TV set under her arm.

One cop comes over and stands in front of us. My cock is bleeding quite a bit. I look up at the cop. I am ready to ejaculate. She digs in harder. I jizz on his shiny black shoes.

He reaches down to grab us but we are too quick. (He has eaten too many donuts.) We run and he does not bother to chase us. Her right hand is sticky with blood and with cum. She runs faster than I do. Her unpolished nails are speckled with red. As we run, she picks up a rock with her gooey right hand and tosses it through the window of a Pizza Hut delivery store.

Now we have done something wrong.

IX.

I am thinking about the armistice and about how much I like parades. Despite the fact that I cannot conjure up a war to go with it, my favorite is St. Patrick's Day. Everybody is drunk and the women on the floats are waving. I take another sip of beer, then bend over to puke in the gutter. The man next to me sings "Give Ireland Back to the Irish." I try to call her but she is not home.

X.

I am already awake when the alarm rings, but I do not get out of bed. Instead I reach for the remote control, then for my cock. The long, thin cuts along the shaft hurt more when it is hard. Blood pressure. I rewind the video to the part where she has one up her ass and one in her pussy.

The scabs are new so my cuts start to bleed again. I lose my concentration looking at the window shade. The holes in it let in too much light. It makes things difficult.

After playing the scene eight times I finally come. My hand is coated with blood and with cum, which I wipe on the sheets. I pull the covers up over my head and go back to sleep.

XI.

The next morning he meets me as scheduled. I wait until he shoots up. He is antsy until the heroin kicks in.

"What are you going to do?" he asks.

"Shoot you," I say.

"Can you make it in the leg?" he asks.

"Alright," I say. "The thigh or the calf?"

"Ah, the thigh, I guess."

The apartment is dingy, unpainted, poorly lit at night, but bright enough by day; I have a good stereo system.

"I'm going to put on some music so no one can hear the shots."

"Shots?"

"I'm sorry," I say. "Just one. One in the thigh."

I put just one bullet in the gun so he believes me.

"You want to hear something special? I've got a lot of tapes."

"Whatever."

"No, you choose."

He doesn't say anything.

"I've got the Grateful Dead."

Silence.

"Sorry. How about Janis Joplin?"

"You got anything new?"

"Soul Asylum?"

"Sounds good."

I put the tape in. I hadn't heard it much. She gave it to me. I stare for a bit at the figures walking away on the cover of the album.

I adjust the volume to his preference. It's the least I can do. I spend a little time at it before he is satisfied.

It is sunny. It is bright. The apartment looks better than I have ever seen it.

LA is the last stop. You run out of country here. You can tell by the sky.

I do it. Close range. I pull the trigger. He yelps. Cries. It is over. I raise my hand in triumph. He smiles wanly. I feel good. He shakes my hand. Together we call an ambulance. He is reluctant to leave. The driver is impatient. Both of us give him a dirty look. We embrace. They put him in a stretcher and carry him out. He is bleeding but he does not really need the stretcher. He tells me this. I smile. Quickly he is gone. I miss him. The place is empty. No one. Nothing. I see the television. I grab the remote control. I want the double penetration scene. I push the buttons. I grab my dick. I want to come. I want to sleep. Hard. Hard. Almost. Right there. Yes. Yes. I want to sleep. Sleep. It has been a long time since I have gotten a good night's sleep. Goodnight.

Stalemate

He had a gun and I had a gun.

My girlfriend and I were living in a run-down place on Grand Avenue near the freeway. They'd just re-opened the Grand Olympic and I got a job selling tickets to the boxing events and the rock concerts.

The guy with the gun just came in off the street. Intent on robbery, I guess. Cheap gun, I noticed.

"Freeze," I yelled, like a cop, and turned on the lights. He had his gun pointed at me already. I was naked but I had my gun out, too.

He laughed when he saw me without clothes and I turned red.

Eileen came out from our bedroom in the back. She saw the two of us with guns.

She screamed and I slapped her—the first time ever.

"He's got a gun," I said.

I had a hard-on. Eileen noticed, came up by my side, and grabbed it.

"Don't fuck with me," the man said.

He waved his gun at me. I waved my gun back at him.

"Do something," Eileen said.

"Put the gun down," I said to him.

"Fuck you," he said. "I'll kill the both of you."

"Kiss my ass."

"Are we all going to die?" he asked.

"It's up to you," I said, feigning bravery.

"It's fine with me," he said.

It went on and on.

Finally, I asked: "You wanna watch a show?"

"Letterman still on?"

"I hate Letterman."

"You watch Leno?"

"Yeah, what about it?"

"He's a fucking pussy. Turn on Letterman."

"Don't tell me what to fucking do."

He fired a shot at the ceiling and I switched on Letterman.

The upstairs neighbor banged on the floor for us to be quiet.

"Fuck you," he yelled.

We watched Letterman for a while and when he found out we had cable, we switched to HBO.

I drive a motorcycle; the night before I'd come home all wet. It was January in Los Angeles, the height of the rainy season. I remembered my sopping clothes were still in the bathtub. Time passed.

Then he said: "I want her to blow me."

I realized Eileen was naked, too. Her nipples were erect in the cold night air.

"Fuck you."

"I'll shoot you," he said.

"I'll shoot you first."

"It's alright," Eileen said.

"What?"

"I'll do it."

She walked over to the stranger, unzipped him, pulled down his pants, got on her knees, and sucked his big cock.

He kept the gun pointed at me the whole time, surprisingly undistracted though Eileen was clearly doing a good job.

I thought of the movie Speed where Keanu Reeves shoots his cop partner to get away from Dennis Hopper who is holding him hostage. The man never took his eyes or his gun off me even when he went off in Eileen's mouth. He shuddered and she swallowed—forcefully and several times. It was clearly a good one.

Eileen rubbed his shoulder with her hand (she has great nails and they feel wonderful) as if to comfort him, and then she moved away from him and sat on the floor midway between us. He stood up to put his cock back in his pants and he zipped up. He was the only one with clothes on. His pants were plaid and a little too short.

He asked if we had any "Medicine" and Eileen thought he had a headache and got up to go to the bathroom and the medicine cabinet. I saw him gesturing towards the stereo system and I knew he meant the band.

"We've got 'The Buried Life,'" I said.

"That's a good one."

"I agree."

"I saw them live," he said.

"At 'Rudolpho's?'"

"Were you there?"

"We both were," I said. Eileen had returned to the room with a bottle of aspirin.

"Where did she go?" he said. "I didn't say you could leave the room." He was shouting now and waving the gun.

"You called the cops, didn't you? you bitch," he screamed.

I took a step towards him with my gun.

"Calm the fuck down," I said. "Remember, we both have guns, asshole."

"I didn't call any one," Eileen said. "We only have one phone." She pointed a long, red nail at the blue telephone on the homemade coffee table, a plate of glass stretched across two piles of red bricks.

"I got you some aspirin," she said. She held up a container of Bufferin. Amidst her long, red nails and pale skin, the white and blue plastic bottle cut a sharp, distinct shape; it looked almost too real. The intruder and I both stared at the medicine in Eileen's hand for a full minute. Eileen kept her arm extended for as long as we looked.

"I don't..." he started, then broke into laughter. I had to laugh with him. We listened to the CD from start to finish.

I got tired before he did. I'd been sitting against the wall. My head started nodding and dropped to my chest. He was sitting against the opposite wall and he did not move. Eileen must have come to sit beside me because that's where she was when I woke up. The gun was still in my hand and her hand was on mine.

Our apartment was bare—little furniture, nothing on the walls. If the police were trying to describe it, they'd have a hard time thinking of what to write.

We all got thirsty. We drank a half-gallon of orange juice among us. We spent a long time looking at each other without noticing much.

In the silence, I thought about Eileen—a model, now a writer and a painter. Smart, but deliberate. I was pretty sure she wouldn't catch on. She looked calm, beautiful, resting but not sleeping in a surprisingly stoic pose.

I tried, but I couldn't figure what Eileen was thinking about. I was certain though that the intruder was thinking about her.

Finally, at around sun-up, he started to doze. He slumped over in sleep and the gun dropped from his hand.

I sprang to my feet.

"Call 911!" Eileen shouted.

"Shhh!" I said. "You'll wake him up."

The man did not stir.

Eileen started for the phone, and I grabbed both her wrists.

"No!" I said.

"What?"

"Don't call the cops."

"You want to tie him up first or something?"

"No," I said.

She looked me up and down.

"We'll be dressed long before the cops get here," she said.

"Eileen, go get your clothes on. I'll stay here and watch him."

"Let's call first. We can get dressed later."

"Eileen, go!"

"Honey..."

"Now!!!" My teeth were shut tight like a jammed door.

She started towards the bedroom. She was muttering, calling me names under her breath, but at least she was moving. I could hear her rattling and slamming the dresser drawers.

I walked over to the intruder, this dipshit asshole slumped against my wall. He was snoring, the dumb-ass.

I kicked him hard in the ribs. It happened quickly like I thought it would. He woke with a startle and instinctively grabbed for his gun. As soon as I figured he had a sufficient grip on it to leave a good, fresh print, I raised my gun and fired. I shot three times—the head, the chest, the stomach—good shots all three times. His body jerked and he splattered blood on my wall and he slumped further to the floor. That was it. He seemed to die right away.

Eileen came running from the bedroom. She had gotten her panties on and her pants, but not a bra or a top or shoes. She was still bare-breasted and barefoot. Her eyes were full of I-don't-know-what. My cock was stirring but not erect.

"He woke up. He grabbed his gun. I had to shoot him, Eileen. I had to." Eileen did not move.

"Don't just stand there," I said. "Call the cops."

By Force

How I Got Her Back

Outside the Powerhouse, the lights were bright; inside it was dim. I hadn't been in a fight for years, but I knew what I was getting into.

I walked right up to her table.

Hello I said.

You bastard she said.

She was going out with a weightlifter now. She had met him at the Hollywood Gym. He looked up at me.

I didn't expect to see you here I lied.

Buy me a drink, she said.

I walked over to the bar and ordered two bourbons. I placed one drink in front of her; I sipped from the other.

Don't you say thank you? I asked.

The weightlifter said: I'm drinking Heineken.

So what I said.

She stirred her drink. Two women in tight leather miniskirts bumped me as they passed by. I turned to look at their asses.

Still the same she said.

Horny I said.

Motorcycles revved outside. (Old friends.) The band came back onto the small stage.

You wanna dance? I asked.

Alright she said, and then she said Excuse me to her boyfriend.

I thought of memories and times we had together, and other sentimental things. (Her tits were big as ever.) When she stood up I saw she had on a short leather skirt too.

New addition? I asked.

I've changed she said.

So I see.

The band covered "Miss You"; poorly I thought, but they had the rhythm right. She still moved well.

When the band slowed it down, and we stayed on the floor, her new guy came over and pushed in on the number.

I'll take this one he said, first looking at me, then at her.

I had on an oxford cloth shirt with a button-down collar, and wing-tip shoes. But I knew every one.

It's up to you I said to her. My arms were still around her shoulders. Her big guy wrenched my elbow from behind.

It was too early.

I'll get us another drink I said. I went to the bar and got us two more bourbons. They were back at the table. The big guy's glass was empty.

Don't you have any money? I asked him.

He squeezed out of the booth and went to the bar for himself. (Round one.)

When he got back, she and I were talking about polar bears.

They make igloos for themselves I was saying.

Really she said.

You know anything about polar bears? I asked him.

He tipped a little beer on my lap as he sat back down.

Are you clumsy? I asked him.

Who is this asshole? he asked her.

I lived with him for six years she said.

I was proud of the acknowledgement.

The motorcycle guys were getting loud. She was sitting between me and her big guy.

Let's go over to Miceli's I said. We can get a pizza.

She said yes, and the big guy looked pissed.

Don't worry I said, it's close by.

She and I stood up.

You coming? I asked the lug. He couldn't think too fast.

He brought the Heineken bottle down on my head. It didn't break. Susie screamed. He and I tussled on the floor for awhile; he was getting the better of me, except I knew the motorcycle guys from way back, and they kept kicking him when we rolled by.

Get him, Tommy, one of them yelled to me when I began beating him with my shoe. I got up and scrambled back to Susie. My nose was bleeding. The big guy was still on the floor and the motorcycle guys were kicking him harder, and then they hit him with a barstool. Susie didn't say a word.

You still want pizza? I asked.

Sure she said. So we slipped out and over to Miceli's. The motorcycle guys were still beating on her boyfriend as we left.

Bank Robber

He stole the money and he put it in the bank. That is he took it from one bank and put it in another. He reasoned it would be safe there. He withdrew it frugally—a little at a time. He committed his first and only robbery in 1940 at the age of 23. He lived quietly in a sparsely furnished apartment. Still he expected to be caught. The years passed. He flinched every time the door bell rang. Wisely, he never got a phone. He read the papers assiduously. He watched both versions of *The Getaway*. Gradually he accumulated seventeen cats. While in his fifties, he met a woman he loved but would not marry for obvious reasons. She was a librarian. He took her out on courtly, old-fashioned dates. He remained celibate for ten years. When he broke his period of abstinence, he used a condom. He never had to work on account of his large deposit. At first he went with a simple passbook account, then he moved into money market funds and certificates of deposit. He began to take risks. His portfolio—he called it that now —grew. Of course he never could have foreseen the S & L and the junk bond crises. At seventy he had to go back into business. The situation had gotten so bad out there that this time he brought along a gun.

Gutless

I started it; I said something wise; I was a smart-aleck. I was sitting at the bar. He came in around my sixth beer. Stood behind me—too close—I didn't like it. He reacted to my wisecrack—invited me outside. I refused to go. Then he started calling me names. Really insulting me. It all added up to calling me a pussy, a wimp, a chicken-shit—in a hundred different ways. I still wouldn't budge.

The place was dark, without windows. It smelled bad—like piss and stale beer. Guys mostly drank beer there, a little whiskey, nothing else. No mixed drinks, no wine. I'd been in there a few times before, but not regular.

When the guy got up to go piss, I left—walked home. Just down San Pedro Street. It was a nice night outside—a bit cool, refreshing. I really needed a sweatshirt, but I walked briskly—got used to it—it felt good.

I came back in about forty minutes. The guy had a seat at the bar by then. I had a 9 mm semi-automatic. I just opened up—hit three or four people, I think—a couple of patrons and the bartender. (The papers said four.) But I got him—got him good—damn near took his head off—not much left, not to speak of anyway.

Take the Fucking Thing

Joe Sparks had bought a lemon. A 1993 Pontiac Fiero. Bright red. He expected to love the car. For the first month, he did.

Then he began to have trouble getting it started in the morning. It would take 15 or 20 minutes. After that it would start great the rest of the day. So, of course, when he took it to the dealer it worked just fine.

Next the transmission went out completely. He'd taken Sarah, the new receptionist, to the Sports Arena for a concert to see Sonic Youth. In the parking lot after the event, the car started but wouldn't go into gear. He had to call Triple-A, get towed, take a cab; it was a mess, ruined his date.

He tried to return the car. They said they'd fix it for him. As soon as they would, something else would go wrong. Time after time. In the first six months he owned the car, Joe had to take it in eight times.

He complained at the dealership; he called the Better Business Bureau; he wrote letters to the Chairman of General Motors.

One night late, driving along Cahuenga, Joe was stopped at a light. A skinheaded young man, about nineteen, approached the driver's side window and smashed it with a crowbar.

"Get out of your car," he said.

It took Joe a minute to think. In the mean time, he glared at the kid and instinctively reached under his seat where he kept a 9mm pistol.

Picking up on the menace in Joe's eyes, the carjacker took a few steps backwards. Joe stepped out of his car, gun in hand.

"Mister, I...I...I didn't," the young man stammered.

Joe pointed the gun at him.

"Take the fucking car," he said.

"What?"

"You heard me," Joe said. "Take the fucking thing. Get in the fucking car and drive it away."

"But."

"Do it!"

"You're going to shoot me."

"I'm going to shoot you if you don't take the fucking car," Joe said.

Biting at his fingers and looking over his shoulder, the young man got

21

into the Pontiac. Joe closed the door for him.

"Go," he said.

The kid hesitated for a moment, then sped away.

Joe smiled and looked around for a pay phone to call a cab. He lit a cigarette. In LA, waiting for a taxi to come can take forever. He wouldn't call the cops until tomorrow, give the kid some time. Then he would wait a few days and, with his fingers crossed, call his insurance company.

Insomnia

Thomas James was walking along in the dark, the streetlights out. Mechanical failure or shot out, one or the other. Dogs barked. His own dog tugged hard at her leash.

"Watch your car?" a voice said from behind a bush, short beside a tall tree.

"I'm walking," Thomas said.

"Five dollars and no one will bother it."

"Don't have a car. I'm on foot."

"Watch your car?" the voice repeated.

"I'm not driving," Thomas said, "I'm on foot."

In the dark Thomas could not see the man who was speaking, but the voice made him tighten his grip on the dog's leash. Sparky strained at her collar.

Thomas looked down. He was standing on a copy of the LA Times that had landed at the edge of a driveway, an early morning arrival, neatly folded for delivery. He shuffled his weight awkwardly in the silence.

There was a faint smell of smoke in the air—something burning far away.

"I'm on foot," he repeated, though he was not asked again. He spoke slowly, emphatically, then began to walk again, stiffly and deliberately, upright, showing his fearlessness.

He gradually picked up his pace, turning left and left again onto Hoover to complete his typical walk back home. By the time he neared his house, Sparky was panting. Thomas must have been running. He moved quickly up his driveway—dark, porchlight on, but dim—his Buick still parked on the pavement. Then he noticed the broken glass gleaming on the asphalt—all four windows, both front and back windshields, smashed, gone, bricks on the seat upon closer inspection with a flashlight. Just broken glass all over.

Thomas took our his house keys and opened the door cautiously. His wife and children were out of town, visiting her parents in Bakersfield. He looked out the window, parting the drapes only slightly, before turning on the light. He stared at the phone—pale blue—for a few minutes. He picked up the receiver, then put it back again. Though he was sitting still, Thomas was still breathing hard. He sat down in the leather loveseat, fished around for the remote control, and turned on the television. He flipped the channel fourteen or fifteen times, but it was four in the morning, there was nothing on.

Hilfiger

The streets of Echo Park were wet and unlit. It had just stopped raining and the lights had gone out in the storm.

One well-dressed man approached another.

"I'll give you five bucks for your watch."

The man with the watch was wearing a long-sleeved shirt that protruded from the sleeves of his jacket—a red, white and blue Tommy Hilfiger windbreaker.

"Five bucks! You got to be kidding."

"Alright, ten."

"It's a fucking Rolex, asshole."

The moon was full over the Stadium. The rain had lasted nearly a week. The Dodgers had just been put up for sale.

"Fifteen's my final offer."

"Fuck off!"

At that, the buyer hit the seller over the head with a baseball bat.

The seller fell to the ground. The buyer proceeded to remove the Rolex from the seller's left wrist. He put the watch in one of his own pockets, and, from another he took out a ten dollar bill and a five. He placed the money into the pocket of the seller's Tommy Hilfiger jacket.

The buyer walked quickly away, but he did not run.

The rain started to fall again.

Cuckold II: A Bar Story

He went down to the bar without windows and put quarters in the juke box.
The regulars looked at him funny because they did not know him.

It was nearly midnight on a dark but hot July night near downtown LA.

The last two things he could remember in the papers were the LA riots and the Gulf War.

She had big tits and she was cheap. He had come twice and she didn't charge him any more. He could have sworn she came, too. She was the best one he ever had. The experience put him in a good mood.

***

"Budweiser, please." That was all the bartender could recall him saying. He had six beers; he said the same thing six times. Nothing else. He always said "please." He never moved from his stool, not even to piss. He did not say "thank you."

The Dodgers lost to the Giants that night.

Joe was on the stool beside him and all of a sudden he just fell to the floor. The knife in his back was up to the hilt but at first you couldn't see it.

He finished his sixth beer a moment after Joe hit the ground. Then he got up and walked out the door all calm and collected like nothing had happened.

The bartender and the regulars figured Joe had a heart attack; he was so big and out of shape. By the time they noticed the blood and the knife, he—you know who I mean—was gone.

Of course there were no fingerprints on the knife. The murder made the KCAL News at six o'clock and it was in *The LA Times* and *The Daily News* the next day but not on the front page.

They never found the guy though the bartender said he once saw him in a phone booth. That must have been, oh, six or seven years ago now.

***

Lessons he learned:

1.) Always go for the ones with the big tits.

2.) The media can help you or hurt you. Unless you really know what you're doing, try to leave them out of it.

3.) Disguises are unnecessary. Most people have terrible memories.

4.) Move out of state for a while. In a few years you can always come back.

5.) Be persistent. In the end, talent, cleverness, ingenuity, etc. all matter less than persistence.

6.) Don't be flashy. A quiet competence is always superior.

7.) Liquor isn't as bad as they make it out to be.

8.) Keep a souvenir. It will bring back memories. No pictures, of course; a camera is out of the question.

9.) Be polite. Good manners go a long way.

10.) Do wear gloves. A foolish carelessness can kill you.

***

His precepts:

Don't let any one take advantage of you.

Don't get mad; get even.

Two wrongs may not make a right, but revenge sure feels good.

If you don't eat, you'll starve.

A stitch in time saves nine.

A penny saved is a penny earned.

A bird in the hand is worth two in the bush.

Don't be penny-wise and pound foolish.

Cleanliness is next to godliness.

Silence is golden.

***

Business picked up for a while after the murder, then fell off considerably. Even some of the regulars stopped coming. The owner said all of this had to do with normal business cycles. Maybe he's right because after he started with a Happy Hour and a Ladies' Night on Wednesdays the crowds started coming back again.

The place looks the same. The same stools are still there—the one the killer was sitting on and the one Joe had occupied. They just washed the blood off. It came off real easy. The legs are chrome and nothing sticks to them that can't come off with a little polish and some elbow grease and the seat is made of vinyl, and, with a little Fantastic it came clean right off, too. Just like new. Of course now no one can tell which is which. There are twelve stools in all. When the janitor comes in at night to clean up he puts all the stools up on the bar to mop the floor and, of course, he doesn't always put them back in the same place. In fact, one time he said—one of the regulars asked—he put all the stools in the bathrooms because he was putting a new coat of polyurethane on the bar the same night he was mopping and he had to do something with the stools, get them out of the way. So the stools are all mixed up, all in different places from where they were the night Joe died. And no one can tell the difference between one and another, no one knows whether they're sitting on the killer's stool, or Joe's stool, or one of the other ten, the ones that nothing happened on.

Driving Cars

Fatal Accident

— Joe —

We had been arguing all night. At three in the morning, she threw me out. Or maybe I left, I can't remember. We fought like people who wanted to, although we'd always swear otherwise.

It was the first cool night of September. A fog hung over La Cienega Boulevard below the Santa Monica Freeway. The moon was almost full and it backlit a billboard advertising Absolut Vodka. I was heading south. A string of planes crossed my path, east to west, heading for LAX. I rolled down the windows and opened the sun roof to let in the cool, fresh air.

First I was up, then I was down. I wasn't paying much attention when a Ford Bronco hit the intersection of Rodeo Road at the same time I did. I don't know who ran the light, but both cars got spun around pretty bad. Smashed the shit out of my Fiero.

I stormed out of the car. The guy was already out of his. I looked at the damage. He didn't. He was holding a gun.

"Hey, wait a minute," I said. "My insurance company will pay for this."

When I thought about it, I figured he had run the light.

He waved the gun in the air, up above his head.

"Really," I said. "I'll give you the information."

He didn't say a word. He steadied the gun and pointed it at his own temple. He pulled the trigger. I watched the explosion, the bullet tearing through his skull and his brain. I knew he was dead.

After I called my girlfriend, I called the cops.

Floored

— Mary Ann —

He was standing at the end of the offramp at Silver Lake Boulevard off the 101. I was one lane away. Above us was the bright green and yellow neon sign of Western Exterminators. He held a cardboard sign. I could not read it all, but I knew what it said: "Homeless. Vietnam Vet. Please help. God bless." I ignored him at first, then turned up the radio. It was a long light. The wind blew litter all around along the asphalt. Trash circled my tires. A sheet of paper stuck to my windshield.

I tried to stare straight ahead. Instead, I looked at his eyes. The light was still red. I fished around for a dollar, took one out of my pocket, opened the window and waved it at him. He wore a bright green sweater.

I realize now that I had waited too long. Seeing the dollar, he ran across the lane that separated me from him. Meanwhile, the light had turned green. The car that hit him never stopped.

Reversal of Roles

— Mark —

My foot slipped off the brake. The car inched forward into the crosswalk. I had a donut in my left hand. I felt the impact as the car slid into a tall thin man crossing the street. I watched my cup of coffee fall from the console onto the carpet. I jammed on the brake. The man fell but picked himself up quickly. It had not rained in months. I was thinking of telling the man that my car had slid on wet oil, but that would have been easy to disprove. I picked up the coffee cup before getting out of the car.

The man was visibly angry. I really did feel bad. I apologized profusely.

"You hit me," he said.

"I am sorry," I said. "It was an accident."

"Pretty fucking stupid, I'd say."

"I am truly sorry, but you don't have to be insulting."

"I should kick your ass."

"Are you hurt?" I asked. In part I was genuinely concerned; in part I just wanted to assess my chances in case this guy got violent.

"Yeah, I'm hurt," he said. "And first, I'm going to kick your ass, then I'm going to sue you."

"Let me get my insurance information," I said.

The LA County District Attorney bellowed on the radio. A Public Service Announcement. After losing the OJ case, the DA was trying to curry voters with a crackdown on insurance fraud.

I leaned into my car and fished around in the glove compartment. A gorgeous woman in a tight miniskirt strolled into the crosswalk. I whistled, but softly so she couldn't hear. I searched around some more in the glove box; I found what I was looking for.

I stood up, a little dizzy from being hunched over for so long, and as soon as I straightened my back, he hit me. First, a punch to the face, then a shot to the stomach.

"Cut the shit," I said. "I didn't mean to hit you. It was an accident."

He wouldn't stop.

"I hate clumsy shitheads like you," he said. "I told you I was going to kick your ass and I'm a man of my word."

He pummeled my face a few more times before I pulled out the gun. I waved it a bit and he stepped back.

"Hey, come on now," he said.

I fired three shots, all at his stomach. They all hit. I could see his grimace tighten as each bullet struck. He lost his feet with the third shot.

I smiled at him as he lay in a pool of blood. I wished he had accepted my apology and I told him that. I moved him onto the sidewalk. I noticed that the girl in the miniskirt was heading back across the street. She was carrying coffee and donuts. I smiled at her and she smiled back. I got back in the car. Only a few people had gathered around. I smiled at them, too. Self-defense, I was trying to say with my expression, innocent and open. I looked down at the floor. My own coffee and donuts had made a mess of the carpeting.

Undesired

He sat down beside me. I did not want to talk.

"Great place," he said—somewhere between an exclamation point and a question mark.

Gwendolyn was grinding her ass nearby.

"Yes," I said as curtly as possible.

It was a funky old strip joint on Hollywood Boulevard. Been there thirty years. The strippers wore pasties on their nipples. Some wore sparkles; some wore electrical tape.

"She's got great tits," he said.

I turned red in the face, but it was too dark for anyone else to tell.

"I'm Eddie." He put out his hand to shake.

I squeezed his fingers together, hard enough to hurt, but I did not say my name.

Gwen bent over, ass in the air, right in front of me. She shook it and stuck it out towards me. I put five dollars on the rail.

"What do you do for a living?" Eddie asked.

"I'm a serial killer," I said.

He laughed. He thought I was kidding. I was not.

Civil Unrest

I want to sit on a chair but there are no chairs.

Sheila is upstairs sitting on the bathroom floor. The floor tiles there are white with intricate scalloped designs. Sheila has always liked them.

Last week we discussed whether the universe is expanding. The next night she slept with some one else.

The Goodwill truck came yesterday and took all the furniture. I am playing the radio in the kitchen. It is not too loud.

I run upstairs to look out off the balcony. The flames are rising on Vermont Avenue. I do not talk to Sheila, who is just a few feet away—still in the bathroom and still sitting on the floor as far as I know.

Sheila and I once went to Florida in August. A bargain vacation. We got a good price, but it was too hot. One day we went to the zoo so the animals could look at us. We wore funny hats, and brightly-colored clothes, and we made silly faces through the bars.

Most of the animals ignored us; many others were asleep. At one cage, where Sheila stuck out her tongue, an energetic mandrill brought his blue face near to the bars and looked back at us. His eyes were black and wet and close together on his face. They looked like drops of water balanced on a wire. The mandrill frowned and held his frown. The patch of red that licked up between his eyes looked like a tongue pasted on his face. His beard was white and neat. His arms were by his side. He kept his eyes on us, and we kept ours on him. When we were all finished, we walked away from the cage, not smiling. I turned around as we walked away; the mandrill was still looking at us. Behind me I could hear him breathing.

On the way out we bought some popcorn.

***

There is no music on the radio, only news. The Mayor has called for a dusk to dawn curfew. We have tickets to see Pearl Jam tonight. I guess it means we cannot go.

The sun is low in the sky. I am hungry. It must be nearly seven. I look at my bookshelf, hundreds of books. I try to read some titles but my eyes are itchy and burning. I have hay fever and all this smoke only makes it worse.

Sheila won't leave the bathroom until much later tonight. That I know for sure. History does teach us some things.

I have switched off the news and put the Grateful Dead in the tape player. My neighbor Art comes over, barefoot and shouting.

"They're looting the Circuit City on Sunset," he says. The store is only a few blocks from our duplex.

"Shh!" I say. "You'll disturb Sheila."

"How can she sleep through this?" he asks, thinking, I guess, that she is in bed.

"She doesn't feel well." I've told this lie for Sheila so many times.

"Oh," he says, unconvinced I am sure.

I think Art wants to go up there. He has been talking lately about buying a VCR.

I offer a comment. "I have to take care of Sheila," I say.

Art leaves, looking disappointed. Next door he turns his television on full blast so I can hear all the stories. I crank up the Dead.

Sheila doesn't want to have children. We have been together nearly ten years. She thinks I should have accepted it by now.

It is nearly dark. I pace around the house making as much noise as I can in an attempt to dislodge Sheila. In the hallway, a poster of Ho Chi Minh falls to the floor. The Scotch tape is old and yellow and no longer sticky. I cannot get the poster to stay back up, so I tuck it behind the bedroom door.

With Sheila I keep thinking "if only." Like on our first vacation when I yelled at her for breaking my glasses. I knew it was an accident, but carelessness has always bothered me. We were in Ensenada. I couldn't find an optician, or I didn't look very hard, I'm not sure which. Sheila had to drive the whole time and all the way back.

I hear cars driving by, horns counting out a beat, breaking glass, loud voices, sirens, helicopters, car alarms.

A mob races down my street, shouting. Though I look for him, I do not see Art. Sheila is still upstairs. I wait for the crowd to pass. Then I walk outside. Alone I pace a few hundred yards back and forth in front of my home. I am screaming at the top of my lungs: "No justice, No peace."

I laugh out loud to myself—long and hard like a crazy man. I think "if only" again and again. I know the social question now; I listened to the news long enough. Out in front of my house I am catching ashes in my hand like butterflies.

When I finish—after about fifteen minutes of continuous shouting—Art has two chairs out on the front porch, a beer set in front of each one.

"Come on, buddy," he says. "Have a beer with me."

The streetlights go out; the power's gone in the neighborhood. I sit down hard, grunting, groping for the beer in the dark. Sheila is still upstairs, or maybe gone by now, I don't know for sure.

Generic Story

She wants more money than I have so I sell my car. I had met her in a bar.

She shows me her tits and why they are special. She makes them up around the nipple with lipstick and rouge, and eyeliner for emphasis. I cannot resist.

We do not talk very much.

We hitchhike to Ensenada and from there to Cabo, stopping in Santa Rosalia and La Paz.

We see her family.

I buy her volumes of make up.

We make great love. I have my savings wired down to me. I spend it all.

I confide all my dreams in her. In a bar I kill a man who tries to rape her.

She does not leave me. I cannot say that. She asks for more money, but I am all out. We just look at each other.

***

After several days of standing around alone in the plazas of the town, begging money and drinking warm beer in the hot sun, I hitchhike back to Los Angeles.

I am standing in an alley off Central Avenue, cooking over a flame blazing in an overturned trash can, talking with a man named Hernando who has built an altar of tin cans and bottles and has fires burning in them at all times.

A heavy-set woman, also homeless, approaches us. She is wearing a halter top and her stomach is bulging below it. She asks for a cigarette. I give one to her. She flashes me a view of her tits. Of course, she has them made up with lipstick and rouge and eyeliner for emphasis.

Bar Story #3

I was behind the bar getting a blow job from Clara, a local hooker and a regular at my place. The joint was empty except for a few other regulars getting smashed. Joey wanted a drink but I was so close to getting off that I told him to fuck off and he left. I think he's sore at me; I haven't seen him since. It was just after I came—I shot really hard in her mouth—when that woman walked in.

"Where's Patrick," she demanded.

"Who's Patrick?" I asked.

"Don't fuck with me." She pulled out a pistol. I was ten feet and a recent jizz away from my shotgun.

"Pull up a stool. Let me buy you a drink. What do you like?"

Clara stood up from behind the bar and giggled. The woman with the gun was big and tall, and bleached blonde, and mean-looking—with a scar near her lips—but she laughed anyway.

"A Rob Roy. Can you make one?"

Her fingernails were four inches long, pointed, and red.

I went into my private stock and pulled out a bottle of Glenlivet, 15 year. I must admit I made her a mean drink. Perfect, just perfect. She sipped once and agreed.

"Put out your hand," she said.

"I told you, it's on me."

"Just do it," she said.

I obeyed.

She scratched the top of my hand quickly and hard and she drew blood.

"Lick your wound," she said.

There were four bloody lines from my wrist to my knuckles. I licked my blood.

"Now, where's Patrick?"

Albert came up to the bar just then and wanted two drafts for himself and his new girlfriend. Albert was homeless for about half of each month. The other half he spent treating some woman he met on the streets just like a queen—or at least as close as you could get to the royal treatment at Main Street and 12th.

While I poured the beers I looked at his woman, squirming in a corner booth, stripped to her bra. This month's flavor was better than usual.

"Nasty cut on your hand there, Bob." Albert paid me, took his beers, and went back to Rocky Road over there.

"Come on now," she said when we were alone again.

"I had to think for a minute. At first I didn't know what you were talking about. We call him Rick."

"Don't bullshit me," she said. "Bob."

"Well I haven't seen him tonight. I can tell you that much."

She ran her long nails through her platinum hair. Short and even, like it had recently been in a crew cut. Jet black roots. Gorgeous.

"You have a juke box in here?"

"Sure," I said. "I'll play you a song. What do you want to hear?"

"You got 'Joan Jett?'"

"Yeah. What else?"

"How about 'Sublime?'"

"One more. You get three for a dollar."

"Kinda steep."

"I'm paying."

"You're a sweetheart."

"How about some blues?"

"'Howlin' Wolf?'"

"That'd be perfect."

I punched in all the songs and returned to keep the bar.

Meanwhile, Evelyn had come over for another round. She was sitting at a table, strictly formica—so easy to clean—with Ralph. Ralph was an eight-time loser. He'd even run for City Council. The 9th District: Skid Row, South Central, and the downtown skyscrapers. I think he got six votes. Evelyn, the old drunk, she'd stayed loyal to him about the past five years. They came in every night and got totally looped. They lived in one of the better hotels on the row. Some people said Evelyn had inherited some money a while back and that the well was still running. I could make their drinks—bourbon and coke and a Vodka Collins—in my sleep. My favorite customers—those who never change.

"Wanna dance?"

'Sublime' does this ska thing and you can really move to it. I used to dance some in Vegas—one of those strip joints for women—and, though that was 15 years ago, I hadn't forgotten all my moves.

Blondie and I hung on tight to each other.

She dug her nails pretty seriously into my shoulders.

"You see that bitch over there?"

"Evelyn?"

"No, asshole. The one in the corner."

"The one with Albert?"

"If that's his name..."

At the guitar solo, she clawed and clutched me extra hard. Her nails did not break. Never, she said.

"Well anyway, I see her."

"She fucked Patrick."

"You got me."

"It's not a question."

The nails clearly were going through my shirt and into the skin. I could feel the blood.

"Okay."

"While we were engaged..."

Our dance had degenerated into turning in circles.

At just the wrong time, Rick walked in.

She didn't see him at first. Her back was turned and I kept it that way.

"Don't fucking worry. I don't hold a grudge against her. It ain't her fault. I want that son of a bitch, Patrick."

I tried to use hand signals behind my back to warn Rick away. He'd been a good customer. But she caught me.

She didn't waste any time. Patrick—or Rick, as we called him—never said a word. She got him good. It was a big gun—I couldn't quite catch the specifics because I dived the hell out of the way—but, as big and strong as she was, it knocked her back several feet when she pulled the trigger. She squeezed off three shots, all meant for St. Patrick, I am sure.

The problem was, she hit the bitch in the corner—quite accidently she assured me. Now, difficulties arose. Women had shot men in my bar before. I always testified in their behalf—not because of any feminist impulses, but because it was good for business. I could say all the violence at my place was honorable and justified. Not this time. A woman had died.

The shootist proposed marriage to me on the spot. I suppose you could convolute a reason starting from that. Double jealousy, I guess. Of course, I didn't go for it. That would have been too easy and that's not the mood I was in.

First, I made her blow me. I had at least that over her now. Plus, Clara's suck job had been hours ago. I came really quickly again. I'd thought I'd last longer the 2nd time, but Blondie was good.

Now, the problem had changed: I turn to mush when I come. In retrospect, Blondie must have known that. I think she'd talked to Clara—leaving so innocent and all. Now I'm sure she was in on it.

Blondie handed me the gun, which I admit, I took voluntarily—without protest and, without thinking at all, really. The cops, of course, saw two dead people and me with a gun in my hand. They concocted an explanation, an accusation in reality, to be sure. I was just so jealous of the woman in the corner that I shot both her and Patrick; they called him by his full name in court. The third shot was meant for Albert, according to the DA, but he'd snuck out quickly. He never showed to say differently. My fingerprints were all there to prove it and, of course, no one had seen anyone else in the bar at all that night. That was all the testimony.

I was convicted of 2nd degree murder—a crime of passion—and sentenced to nine years.

Blondie married me in a prison ceremony.

Dark; Dirty

"What do you give a shit?"

"I want her."

The glass broke against the wall.

She's big, tall, blonde. She wants to fuck; I can tell.

I have a sports car.

"Hard. She's hard."

I have tattoos, but she has scars.

The music, the sweat—like hands, they push me towards her.

The man she's with is crawling on the floor.

The peppers they keep in the jar are hot. I like them.

She's so skinny I could put my cock between her hips.

They've turned the music up. The cops just walk through. A clubbing occurs. The man's in his twenties. I'm not sure how he's doing.

"She's never been raped."

I don't talk much. I grunt. She seems to know what I'm saying. Gauchos on the pampas have small vocabularies. Less than a hundred words, I've heard. Like dolphins and whales, they communicate with clicks. Something to do with how sound travels.

"What's your name?"

I have nothing to hide, so I tell her. Of course, I know hers.

There are bars on the windows. It is East Hollywood.

"Crime is a problem here. We can't do anything about it."

I've been coming here since I was a kid.

Her skirt is short and leather. I know her ex-husband.

"I think he's in jail."

I like to have advisers.

My cock is stiff. I have children. I'm not sure they'd approve.

The smoke is so thick I'm not sure I can see her anymore.

She wears black spike heels. The spikes are made of metal.

"A shot and a beer, please. Yes, another one."

He smashes the light bulb with his fist. I think he's bleeding.

The waitress wants to know what I want. She sneers, then spits at me, when I tell her I ordered from the bartender.

"We haven't had a shooting in here for a long time."

But I know that. That's not the point.

The motorcycles are parked inside.

She has red hair now, not blonde.

"He's a dangerous motherfucker."

I've been duly warned.

I spent a lot of money. In the past. Put it on the credit card.

"You can't let go."

I find the color of her clothes menacing. They are not black.

Everything's long distance.

She grips with her fingernails, not her fingers.

The graffiti spells words I can't read. Maybe it's in Spanish.

"I'll pray for you." He's a believer. I am too to my surprise. Just not at moments like this.

Dark; dirty. That's how her place was.

She misses. I laugh. What she asks is not too hard. I'm ready to do it. I do it. I'm not sure I'm any the worse for it. I'd do it again. I'm sure of that.

Lone Enemy

I. Grammar

The English teacher worked at night at Greenblatt's Deli.

The young man ordered a ham and cheese sandwich. The English teacher was cheery about it. Customers were few and far between on the graveyard shift; they broke up the boredom.

The deli has a whole section of fine wines and spirits.

"What kind of bread do you want?"

"What you got?"

"White, wheat, rye and sourdough."

"Rye."

The English teacher got the ham from the glass case and brought it over to the slicer. He took pride in slicing the meats perfectly thin—for tenderness and the best taste. Regular customers told him his sandwiches just melted in their mouths.

"Mustard and mayonnaise?"

"I don't want none of that shit."

The English teacher had begun slicing the ham by that point.

The emergency room physicians took six hours to re-attach the thumb.

II. Airplane Fun

It seemed easy to start the planes. Not so different from hotwiring a car.

It was a small airport, in Torrance, California.

Billy got it moving. A Cessna or something. He hurtled down the runway. Some workers there figured out he was trying to steal the plane.

They started shouting. I'm not sure how they knew, but there was nothing they could do about it anyway.

I don't think he was really going that fast, judging by his injuries at least. He crashed the plane into a chainlink fence without ever leaving the ground. The aircraft got messed up pretty bad, but considering the possibilities, Billy came out great—a broken leg, one broken arm and a broken rib. He still hasn't gone to court yet on the charges, but he said he had fun.

III. Searchlights

All I wanted to do was to buy a button hook. I searched all over town —to no avail.

IV. Decisions, Decisions

The light turns yellow. He equivocates: floor it or slam on the brakes. He decides to stop. He stops. The guys have guns. They put them up to the windows. He gets out. They club him on the top of his head (he is bald) with the butts of their guns (two of them do). They drive away in his car.

V. Fingernails

I was driving in the center lane minding my own business when she pulled up beside me. While I'm driving on the freeway—in heavy traffic— I usually look left and right to check out who's driving next to me. I almost always do. Sometimes you catch people picking their noses; many women use the stop-and-go conditions as a chance to touch up their make-up. Young guys shout out the rock songs they're listening to on the radio—you can see their lips move. When you stare at them, as I do—my neck turned fully so it's clear I am looking at them, not just absent-mindedly at my surroundings—they tend to look away.

In the car to my right, the driver—the only occupant, in fact—had the longest fingernails I'd ever seen. They had to be a good ten inches long, on each and every finger and thumb, and they were painted bright green and appeared to be adorned with jewelry—rings and charms drilled into and pasted upon the nails. As we moved from a stop to perhaps 20 mph, I kept my car exactly abreast of hers, staring at her hands the whole time, almost rear-ending the guy in front of me when traffic stopped again.

Needless to say I am a long fingernail fanatic. Have been ever since I was nine years old. I remember my third grade teacher had hugely long nails and she kept them sharp. She pinched me once for talking in line, pulled me over to a corner; for a walk of about ten yards her sharp nails dug into my arms the whole time. I spent the rest of third grade trying to get pinched. Succeeded a good half dozen times. A year and a half later she was my first consummated autoerotic fantasy.

I stayed parallel with the nail queen for a few miles, all the time staring as much as I could. After a few minutes, she noticed. At first she smiled. I pointed to my own fingertips. She knew what I meant and waved her right hand in the air, moved first one finger, then another, the giant nails like razor clam shells, like long, sharpened pencils at the ends of her fingers. (Because of their elongated shape and sharpness, Razor clams, Ensis directus, can dig and burrow faster than any other mollusk.)

She was driving a Mazda Miata, a convertible with the top down. Traffic stopped once again. I could talk to her.

I rolled down the automatic window on the passenger side of my car, a Buick Skylark.

"Great nails," I shouted.

"Thank you," she said.

"I love long nails," I said. "Would you mind pulling over for a few minutes so I could get a closer look at them?"

"That's okay."

"Please. I'm a real admirer. Besides, we're not getting anywhere fast in this shit." I waved my own hand at the bumper-to-bumper back-up of cars.

"For just a minute," she said.

She signaled and began to move towards the shoulder, and I followed right behind her. I tailgated her and kept coming real close so she wouldn't stop near the call box.

KNX said it was a Sig-Alert. We were on the Santa Monica Freeway, heading east, between La Brea and Crenshaw.

She let me touch them. I stroked them, each one, from the base to the very tip. I felt them front and back. I ran my fingertips along the points. I asked to kiss them. She said yes. I went through them one-by-one; I used my lips, my teeth - oh, so gently - and my tongue. Then she said it was time to go. I just couldn't.

"Can I have your number?"

"No."

"I've just got to see you again."

"I've got to go."

"Please."

"You're making me uncomfortable."

"I don't mean to."

"You do."

I grabbed her purse from the front passenger seat of her Miata.

"You're going to rob me?"

"No."

I fished around, found her wallet, rummaged through it, found her driver's license and her checkbook. I compared the addresses. They were the same. I grabbed a piece of paper and jotted down her name and address. Her phone number was printed on her checks. I wrote that down, too. I put everything back.

"I'll call you," I said. "Or stop by."

She looked at me funny; that's how I'd describe it.

The traffic had cleared quite a bit. Not a Sig-Alert; the traffic gurus had changed their verdict. I roared down the breakdown lane for a while, signaled left, then blended into a slow, but steady lane of traffic.

VI. Trucks

The flatbed truck was open in the back. It was stuffed with tools and pipes and boards—nothing strapped down, all bouncing up and down as the truck clattered through the potholes. I was following the truck closely, in heavy traffic. Nervous about the stuff sliding off the flatbed and through my windshield, I dropped back a bit—put a few carlengths between us. A white Mercedes passed me on the left, then cut right in front of me, placing itself between me and the truck.

Where two lanes merged the truck hit the brakes—probably a bit harder than necessary if the truth be known. But the Mercedes was right on his ass.

As the truck came to a halt, and just before it began to accelerate again, a big piece of pipe darted off the back and crashed right through the windshield, driver's side, of that Mercedes. I was still the next car back. Just luck, I guess. The news called it a fatality.

VII. Louis XVI

All year the buzz is about the two Versailles—the Getty Center on the Westside and the Disney Concert Hall downtown.

Meanwhile, at the end of nearly every freeway offramp in the City you encounter a trio of new entrepreneurs: one, usually Latino, is selling bags of oranges and peanuts to passing motorists; a second, most often Black, is asking to wash your car windows; the third, typically white, carries a sign:

"Veteran. Will Work for Food."

I wait tables/do construction (on the subway). I'm in between. There aren't too many of us left.

VIII. Eyes

I was just staring out into space, daydreaming if you will, not looking at anything in particular.

He didn't see it the same way; he obviously thought I was looking at him.

"What the fuck are you looking at, motherfucker?" he asked me as he brought the club down on my head.

IX. Cheap

I look closely and see that urine has permanently discolored the white bowl of the toilet we bought at Sears and I wish that we had bought beige or green when we had the money.

X. Pictures

Cartier-Bresson said there is a decisive moment. I know there is.

I went out each day to dig my part of the hole a little deeper, the hole we were digging daily right outside the post office. Only one person seemed to notice. But, Tutor-Saliba had gone belly-up. You did what you had to do.

Every day, just as regularly, a scraggly old man, the oldest man in the neighborhood, hunched over in a black trench coat, a cane in one hand, his camera in the other, snapped my picture. He said nothing, but he was always there no matter what time of day I arrived. At first I tried to vary my schedule to avoid him. To no avail. But then, not to worry, he has been taking pictures of everyone lately.

Animal Rights

I went to the animal rights demonstration. This fancy restaurant in Beverly Hills was serving hippo meat as a delicacy. (A hundred bucks a plate.) That didn't seem right.

On the way home I was accosted by a man with a pit bull. He demanded money of me. When I refused, he sicced his dog on me. It got a hold of my left ankle and calf and started tearing away the flesh. It had just turned dark. We were at a bus stop on Little Santa Monica. There were a few people around, not many, mostly young women from the protest.

"Call off the dog," I said to the owner, who did not respond.

The women screamed as the dog continued grinding at my leg.

I pulled out a pistol.

"Call off the motherfuckin' dog," I shouted.

The owner remained silent.

I pulled the trigger—two shots to the man's forehead—but the dog did not stop.

I hesitated a moment. The women continued screaming. One brave soul tried to pry the dog away; her hand got bitten badly.

Now, I don't feel pain much. It's not a macho thing; there's just a little something wrong with my brain, with—you know—the receptors for that sort of feeling.

Finally, with little choice and with great regret, I shot the dog. He died instantly, humanely.

A couple of people came over and gently picked up the carcass of the dog. A couple more came to me to tend to my injuries.

The women consoled me:

"You had to do it."

"We saw you hesitate."

"We know you didn't want to (kill the poor thing)."

"There are no bad dogs, only bad owners."

"You and the dog are both victims."

I didn't think they were saying these things just to make me feel better. I agreed with them, but, man, I felt bad about killing that dog.

After I was released from the hospital and put on probation for a weapons violation, I agreed to do my community service hours at the local pound.

Accidents

It was a hot day in September. The white and pink and salmon-colored buildings of Los Angeles seemed to sweat in the sun. I was standing at a bus stop.

"I'm concerned about the money," she said.

I didn't know her and I wasn't sure she was talking to me, so I didn't answer her.

"The money," she said. It was clear now that she was talking to me. That's what I thought. That she was talking to me, for some reason, about money.

She wore short, black hair and a black, lycra tank dress. She was very thin and very attractive.

She did not wear high heels.

The bus stop became crowded with people and the street became busy with traffic. It was late in the afternoon and still in the nineties. The sun was setting, low in the sky and pointing straight at my eyes like a gun.

She had been pacing about and now she was standing still.

"I have some extra money," I said. "Perhaps I can help."

She ignored me.

The bus stop backed up to an automated teller. People lined up behind us to withdraw money from the bank.

"The money," she repeated.

Now I was not sure if she was talking to me or talking to herself or to no one in particular. She was not the type to talk to herself. At that time I knew that. I could tell that. From the context, from the way her eyes worked.

I leaned out over the curb to see if a bus was coming. I had been waiting for a long time.

"You have no idea what I'm talking about." This time, she was clearly talking to me.

The bus, which was clearly late, sped towards the curb. A dog jumped out from among us. I had not seen the dog. There was no way the bus could stop.

The woman screamed and jumped into my arms. The crowd was all abuzz. The dog was obviously dead. It had made a mess. The driver was out of the bus, nervous and upset. You could tell he felt bad about it. The police came but there was no owner, no one to claim the dead animal.

The ReadyTeller line had grown in length.

The woman let go of me.

Another bus came. It was her bus. It was not mine.

She got on it.

I stayed behind.

As her bus drove away, I could see small eyes peering from the back window. There were children at the back of the bus. They were probably thinking about the dog, which was still on the street.

A truck from the Animal Control Department arrived to take the dog away. They had a shovel and they scooped it into a plastic bag. They zipped up the bag and put it into the back of their truck. Then they drove away.

The sun was nearly down. The air had not cooled off much. The line at the ReadyTeller remained long.

Another dog came by, and then another woman. Then a woman and a man. And then, still another dog. Then four men, a cop on a horse, and a butterfly. Bus passengers and bank customers. Then finally a woman with black hair carrying a chicken in a cage.

Meanwhile, six pigeons—a full half-dozen—waddled in the gutter in search of food.

I was standing at a bus stop on a hot evening in Los Angeles, first planning, then not planning, to go anywhere at all. Suddenly I decided to spend all my money—perhaps to search for the woman in the lycra tank dress, perhaps not—to follow the bus in any case. I flagged a cab. The sun set. I was on my way.

Little Things

I was going to the laundry room. A small structure—outside, in back of my apartment building—with a washer and a dryer and a water heater. I grabbed some quarters from a jar of change that I kept on my dresser and stepped into my shoes, crushing down the backs, not troubling to lace them. Why bother? I had only a little way to walk.

It was cold, a night wind, so I hurried down the stairs. I had forgotten my key, but the laundry room door was open. I pulled my things from the washer, sorted out a couple of sweaters to line dry, then stuffed the rest in the dryer.

On my way across the parking area to the stairs to my apartment, I heard some one behind me. I turned around, expecting to see a neighbor.

A strange man in dirty clothes rushed toward me. He did not have a mustache. (I told the police I was sure of that.)

Give me some fucking money he said.

All's I have are these quarters I said, opening my fist to show the coins in my palm.

That's not enough he said.

I saw him reach inside his jacket. He lunged at me.

I turned to run. I heard him chasing me. I had a step on him, and I'm not slow on my feet. Then I stumbled. (As I said, my shoes were not on properly.) He knelt down on top of me and slipped a blade, a kitchen knife, I think, into my side. I felt it against my rib.

He stood over me, a leg on either side. He licked the blade of his knife.

Next time, have some money for me, asshole, he said.

I guess he didn't mean to kill me.

When he bent to put his cigarette out against my face, I bit his wrist. I felt my teeth against his bone, and I moved my jaw side-to-side to grind it. He screamed, and my neighbors came out at that point.

What happened? they asked.

My assailant ran and they watched him run. By that time, the ground all around me was wet with blood. I couldn't stand up.

When the paramedics came, I asked them to find my shoes, which of course had fallen off while I was running.

Make-Up

She was standing at the mirror, putting on make-up. I came up behind her. She saw me, but she did not see the knife I held in my hand. But then, I never saw the gun she kept in her cosmetics drawer, right next to the lipstick, the eyeshadow, the bottles of nail polish.

Deportation at Breakfast

The signs on the windows lured me inside. For a dollar I could get two eggs, toast, and potatoes. The place looked better than most—family-run and clean. The signs were hand-lettered and neat. The paper had yellowed some, but the black letters remained bold. A green and white awning was perched over the door, where the name "Clara's" was stenciled.

Inside, the place had an appealing and old-fashioned look. The air smelled fresh and homey, not greasy. The menu was printed on a chalkboard. It was short and to the point. It listed the kinds of toast you could choose from. One entry was erased from the middle of the list. By deduction, I figured it was rye. I didn't want rye toast anyway.

Because I was alone, I sat at the counter, leaving the empty tables free for other customers that might come in. At the time, business was quiet. Only two tables were occupied; and I was alone at the counter. But it was still early—not yet seven-thirty.

Behind the counter was a short man with dark black hair, a mustache, and a youthful beard, one that never grew much past stubble. He was dressed immaculately, all in chef's white—pants, shirt, and apron, but no hat. He had a thick accent. The name "Javier" was stitched on his shirt.

I ordered coffee, and asked for a minute to choose between the breakfast special for a dollar and the cheese omelette for $1.59. I selected the omelette.

The coffee was hot, strong, and fresh. I spread my newspaper on the counter and sipped the mug as Javier went to the grill to cook my meal.

The eggs were spread out on the griddle, the bread plunged inside the toaster, when the authorities came in. The grabbed Javier quickly and without a word, forcing his hands behind his back. He too, said nothing. He did not resist, and they shoved him out the door and into their waiting car.

On the grill, my eggs bubbled. I looked around for another employee —maybe out back somewhere, or in the wash room. I leaned over the counter and called for someone. No one answered. I looked behind me toward the tables. Two elderly men sat at one; two elderly women at the other. The two women were talking. The men were reading the paper. They seemed not to have noticed Javier's exit.

I could smell my eggs starting to burn. I wasn't quite sure what to do about it. I thought about Javier and stared at my eggs. After some hesitation, I got up from my red swivel stool and went behind the counter. I grabbed a spare apron, picked up a spatula and turned my eggs. My toast had popped up, but it was not browned, so I put it down again. While I was cooking, the two elderly women came to the counter and asked to pay. I asked what they had had. They seemed surprised that I didn't remember. I checked the prices on the chalkboard and rang up their order. They paid slowly, fishing around their large purses, and went put, leaving me a dollar tip. I took my eggs off the grill and slid them onto a clean plate My toast had come up. I buttered it and put it on my plate beside my eggs. I put my plate at my spot on the counter, right next to my newspaper.

As I began to come back from behind the counter to my stool, six new customers came through the door. "Can we pull some tables together?" they asked. "We're all one party." I told them yes. Then they ordered six coffees, two decaffeinated.

I thought of telling them I didn't work there. But perhaps they were hungry. I poured their coffee. Their order was simple: six breakfast specials, all with scrambled eggs and wheat toast. I got busy at the grill.

Then the elderly men came to pay. More new customers began arriving. By eight-thirty, I had my hands full. With this kind of business, I couldn't understand why Javier hadn't hired a waitress. Maybe I'd take out a help-wanted ad in the paper tomorrow. I had never been in the restaurant business. There was no way I could run this place alone.

Fifty-five Word Story

I had been working ten hours straight. Thanksgiving weekend—air travel's busiest.

The tall man put his bag on the belt. I thought the x-ray looked suspicious. No, I'm just tired -- so much luggage today. I let it go.

At home I saw the TV coverage of the hijacking—the dead bodies, the police stand-off.

Weeds

Weeds grew along the outside of the fence. I had to cut them down. Then I cut the metal.

She drank her beer from the bottle, not a glass. Her breasts were small, but firm.

"Will you do it for me?" she asked.

At first it was novel. For that reason only, it was fun.

I like music only when it is loud.

The times with her grew more demanding.

In the basement of a vacant building I made a deal.

I went to bars alone, preferably to places with a live band. Sometimes I winced with the pain.

She was truly beautiful and she studied physics.

"I find women difficult," I said.

"But I'm so easy to please," she said.

Before I met her I drove a truck. Still I had managed to save ten thousand dollars. Within two weeks I had placed the money in her account.

I made a list of the things in my life now. It was a short list; all the old things were gone.

In the mornings I got up a half hour before she did to draw her bath.

Sometimes she preferred I didn't eat.

Her hair was red as candy.

I refused to think conceptually. I accepted the end of philosophy.

She began to reject my overtures.

"I don't enjoy it," she said. "I enjoy the other, which you are getting very good at, by the way."

She kissed the side of my head, just above the temple.

At first there was a purpose, a point to the whole thing.

She wore fewer clothes now and more jewelry.

I rarely left the house.

Then eventually: "Not in my presence," she said.

"When?"

"With me, you do just the other."

We ran out of my money and hers.

Her tone became harsher.

I worked harder for her.

She was losing weight. She thought it was better.

The house was very nice—tile and marble and brass—but too large, she thought, for just the two of us. She wanted to develop a community— of people who did just what we did.

I became successful at making deals, so there was money again.

But for the trappings of her role, she was nude most of the time now.

She wanted more baths and it took me a long time to bathe her.

The days began to seem long.

Her voice grew weak.

I could get in there for her; I knew that. It was just a matter of cutting the fence. I could never say no to her; that's all there was to it. Especially near the end.

Yet it wasn't until I heard the sirens that I really knew it was over.

Stolen Goods

Part One: Free Time

I watched the robber come into the room and steal Martha's purse. We were staying in a nice hotel, somewhere near Los Cabos. I can't remember exactly.

It was very hot, some time in August. I didn't say anything. He acted like he didn't see me.

I went down to the bar and ordered tequila. I charged it to the room, though I no longer knew how we would pay for it. Our credit card was in Martha's purse. I thought there was a number to call.

From the bar, which was open-aired and breezy, I watched the sunset. The azure, the hot pink, all the colors they told us about at the travel agency, they all were there.

Martha was in the pool. I could see her, standing in water up to her waist, talking to a fair-skinned man. They could not see me.

I ordered a second tequila, this time with a Dos Equis.

"A que hora la restaurant abierto?" I asked in my broken Spanish. I wanted to eat alone.

I ate seafood and talked to no one except the waiter. The food and the service were excellent. The white linen tablecloth and napkin were starched and spotless. The silverware was real. I was the only customer eating alone.

Martha and I met back at our room at ten. She was on the phone with security. Her shoulders were considerably sunburned. She was speaking in Spanish.

"You know what happened, don't you?" she said when she got off the phone.

"Yes," I said.

"The door was wide open."

"It happened before that," I said.

She showered and changed. Her hair seemed to lighten in just the few short days we had been here. I nuzzled her and she rebuffed me.

"Are we still going to the nightclub?" I asked.

"The wire's not coming through until tomorrow," she said.

"I still have some cash," I said. "I'd like to spend all mine."

"Are you going to change?" she asked.

"I'll put some new pants on."

She looked so wonderful in her short spandex skirt and heels. I was tempted to tell her that I didn't deserve her, but I kept my mouth shut.

We had rented a small red Volkswagen beetle. I opened the door for Martha and she stretched her long legs into the small area on the passenger side of the car. I ran my hand along her shoulder as she got in. She was still upset with me.

I drove too fast to the center of town. We rode in complete silence. The car had no radio and Martha would not speak to me. About halfway to town I hit something. Martha said it was a cat. I did not see it and I did not hear it and I did not stop. I don't think it was a cat.

In town we parked at a broken meter and beside a high curb. It was too late for meters anyway, but the thing had its top chopped off like a head. Martha had trouble getting out of the car and onto the high curb in her heels so I helped her. The streets were unpaved and untraveled at this hour— empty and dusty and hard to walk on in fancy shoes so Martha took them of and walked barefoot, dust covering first her insteps and then her freshly painted red toenails.

At the club we waited in a short line. Martha put her shoes back on. She seemed excited. She had wanted to come here. I had not heard of the place.

Inside we sat in wicker chairs at wicker tables. Martha slipped her shoes off again and put her feet in my lap. I wiped the dust off her nails and soles and insteps and kneaded her arch. She purred a bit, then leaned over and kissed me. I ordered two Margaritas and moved my chair closer to Martha's.

The band hadn't started yet; a deejay played rhythm and blues. Martha was jumpy now like she had taken speed, though I knew that she would not do that. I danced with her twice, then wanted to sit down. She protested, but sat back down with me. I ordered new drinks.

"Don't you love it here?" she asked.

I was supposed to say yes. "It's great," I said.

"You know, down here, I'm not worried about anything," she said.

"Have you seen the papers?"

"No," she said.

"Should we get some nachos?" I asked.

"I'm not hungry, but get some if you want."

"I don't want to eat them by myself."

"I'll have a few."

"Okay," I said.

"I'll bet they're good here."

"You're probably right," I said.

We stopped talking while I looked for a waiter. Then I started again.

"Martha, I don't understand you. One minute the boy's with us. The next minute he's gone."

"He's better off with his father."

"I don't think you really believe that."

"It's true," she said.

"His father hasn't seen him in five years."

"That was then. This is now," she said. "Things change."

"Yes, they do, Martha," I said. "But you're not fooling any one."

"I'm going to the bathroom. I'll be right back," she said.

I nodded and kept looking for the waiter. All of a sudden I was very hungry.

"Quiero nachos," I said.

"I'll bring some right away," the waiter said.

The nachos came quickly but Martha hadn't returned from the bathroom. I looked around. She was on the dance floor. She was with someone; a man from here in town I guessed. He was smiling and so was she.

They danced again and again. I watched them intently, losing sight of them only now and then amidst the crowd on the dance floor. While I looked, I ate the nachos hurriedly. A fine grease from the cheese and the chips covered my fingertips. I wiped it on my pants.

Martha came back to the table sweaty and carrying her shoes.

"You were gone a long time," I said.

"A guy who lives here, he asked me to dance, and I knew you wouldn't mind, you know how much I like to dance, and how much you hate it," she said. "And besides, he invited us to go out on his boat with him tomorrow."

"I got you a drink," I said. "The ice has melted, but I'm sure it's still good."

She took a sip.

"It is," she said. "I'm very thirsty."

"I'm going to the bathroom," I said. "I'll be right back."

She smiled and gulped the rest of the warm Margarita.

The bathroom, like the rest of the club, was painted in shades of salmon. It was clean and the floor was carpeted. The furnishings were wicker—a tissue box, the wastebasket, and a small chair for waiting.

On my way back to the table I saw three young blondes skip down the stairs into the place, giggling in their short leather skirts, their high heels without stockings, and their bustiers. One was flat, she had nothing on top, but she was, for some reason, the sexiest. My stomach clenched for a short second.

"That was quick," said Martha. She stood up. I sat down. She sat in my lap. She ran her nails along my back, inside my shirt. "Are you ready to go?"

"I was just starting to like it here."

We decided to stay for another drink. I couldn't let her off so easy. I hated it when she punished me.

We were headed for the door, the waiters nodding to us graciously—
"Buenes tardes," "Hasta manana"—when we ran into a couple from our
hotel. They wanted us to stay. They offered to buy.

They were younger—about 25. They ordered tequila slammers for the
four of us. Donna had platinum blonde hair. Hank was shorter and boyish.
He said he played in a rock band, someone I had never heard of.

After the club closed we gave them a ride home as they had taken a
cab.

***

In the morning, I got up first and went down to breakfast alone.

The man who I had watched take Martha's purse was eating eggs and
tortillas at a table by himself. I went over to the table and gestured, asking
without words if I could join him.

I ordered fruit and a margarita. I smiled a lot at the man and spoke to
him in English. He spoke back to me in Spanish. He did not smile so much
as I did. I believe we each understood most of what the other had to say.

We lingered over our food and drink—he was drinking juice. Then,
Martha came down. She was wearing a bikini. I called to her and asked her
to sit down.

I couldn't let her get to me.

"Martha, this is the man who stole your purse."

Martha smiled at me, sat down next to him, and began to speak rapidly
in Spanish.

I could not follow the conversation, but they seemed to be enjoying one
another.

They talked for a long time. I began to get uncomfortable, not
understanding much, and started to rattle the silverware and my margarita
glass.

Martha stood up first. "We better go," she said. She looked at the man.
"It was nice talking with you." She said it in English. She took my hand as
if to help me up from the table. I smiled at the man and said goodbye in
Spanish.

Martha was effervescent. With her she had flat open shoes and a short
jacket.

It was eleven-thirty or so now and already hot.

"Let's take a walk," Martha said.

***

We walked beyond the broken houses, the dusty streets, the garbage
in gutters. After another half-mile of nothing, we spotted an old factory—
abandoned and decrepit. A hungry dog stood still before it like a sentinel.

He barked half-heartedly as we approached and he ran away.

Inside, we rummaged through bottles and metal parts to machines we could not guess. The sign outside was so worn we could not read what once went on there. I took a bottle of wine out of the bag I was carrying and we drank it amidst the debris.

When we finished the wine, we set out running up the hill. The sand quickly filled our shoes and we had to stop to take them off. In the silence we heard the sound of small animals scurrying at our presence.

"I'll race you," she said.

Before she finished her sentence I was running. Breathless, I reached the top of the hill just ahead of her.

It was mid-day - probably 110 degrees. The vegetation was all scrub and cactus, close to the ground. No shady place at all. We were covered with sweat.

"I don't feel drunk," she said.

"It's running down our bodies," I said.

"The bugs like it," she said. She swatted her arms several times.

"Sand fleas."

On both sides of us you could see the ocean. The baja was only 17 miles wide above Los Cabos. South, of course, and straight, there was nothing until Antarctica.

She stripped off her clothes without notice, but I could tell it was not because of desire. She wanted to be a part of it all. Wherever she was she wanted to feel connected to that place and time—to be different, to be of it, to change with the locale: slinky at nightclubs, naked in the desert, hot in Mexico, cold in New York. I did not share that joy in transforming myself so I stood and watched and waited for it to be over, nodding my head when she began to speak.

"Isn't this wonderful," she said. "We're at the end of the earth."

She took my hands to dance with her. I went along with it. She kissed me. I enjoyed her lips though we were both so dry. Suddenly we began to laugh; it started almost simultaneously. I pushed her away long enough to remove my clothes. We held each other again and fell into the sand, laughing still.

Just as suddenly, we stopped. She got up and dressed quickly, not bothering to wipe the sand from her body. I followed suit, but a little more deliberately.

"We better get back," she said.

We walked down the hill and back towards town in silence.

***

On the way back, at the outskirts of town, on a street of adobe and tin and dust, eleven men were gathered in an open field. The field was strewn with old tires, with beer cans and soda cans, and with the bones of dead animals, mostly chickens, the remnants of dinners eaten there in the course of the summer.

The men were squared off, and shouting at one another. It was seven against four. Two men—one from each side—stepped into the middle and began to fight. One was young and short and heavy. He was stripped to the waist and covered with sweat and with dirt. The other was older and very thin. They fought bare-handed.

Martha and I stopped to watch. It was not much of a fight. More words than blows were exchanged; no real punches were landed. The men began to grapple in close, to wrestle upright. Then they stepped back and away from one another.

Standing alone, the younger man grabbed his chest and his throat. He writhed on his feet, then hit the ground. He made no sound; there was no blood. The others closed in on his fallen body, staring intently down at him. The thin man at first had appeared jubilant, then he began to cry. Another man bent down and felt for a pulse. He breathed into the man's mouth.

"Esta muerto," he pronounced to the group.

For the past few moments, I had been pulling on Martha's arm. Martha resisted. She continued to watch closely. When it was over, the dead man still on the ground, the others standing flat-footed, wondering what to do, Martha shouted something at the men. I did not understand what she said.

The men glared at her and at us. She glared back and said it again, this time in a louder voice. Three men started toward us. They were barefoot.

Martha began to run and I followed her. After a few seconds, I did not hear any sounds behind us. I looked over my shoulder. There was no one. The men were back at the field hoisting the body up onto their shoulders. Martha and I slowed from our run, but continued to walk briskly.

We were silent for a long time, but then I asked her.

"What did you say to them?"

"I am not going to tell you."

I started to argue.

"But Martha..."

"I said no," she said. "It would do no good to tell you."

"That's your standard bullshit," I snapped.

"And yours?" she asked.

It was no use. We walked the rest of the way back to town without speaking. We would never talk about it again. It was always like that. It was her way, and it had become mine too, I guess.

As a teenager I boxed at the YMCA. It felt good to hit and get hit. I've never known power without violence. With Martha, with women, I had no idea what to do. Not then and not now.

It was near seven o'clock now and starting to get cooler, but not much. A horde of small children raced by us on rickety bicycles. Five or six dogs followed them. They moved like a cavalry regiment.

We began to see the tourists again along Calle Morelos, but only near the corner, where the restaurants and the shops took over and changed everything.

I changed, too. Mexico is good like that. You can adopt it in your mood. This time, I started the conversation with Martha. I started afresh, as if nothing had happened, and in a way, nothing had. Nothing ever did. Not the way we lived our lives.

Years ago, before we had children, my first wife Eileen and I flew up to Klamath and Crescent City to eat salmon and to be north and in the woods. We drank pale ale in a small loggers' bar in Scotia. We were in love. On the way back, we flew into San Francisco on a twin engine turbo prop with eight seats. Just outside SFO, one of the engines blew. The plane came in off the bay spitting and stuttering. A hard wind was blowing and the plane tilted viciously. Eileen wept on my shoulder. I said nothing. I remember stroking her hair almost absently. My only fear is of being alone.

Martha stroked my hair. Her nails tingled my scalp.

"Let's go down to the water," I said.

"Yes," she said. "We can watch the sunset."

"That's a good idea. It's almost time."

I took Martha's hand. She laughed mischievously. I kissed her briefly and on the cheek. A hotel van stopped in front of a popular bar. Six men in their twenties got out. Already drunk, and dressed in athletic shorts and college t-shirts. They were speaking loudly to each other.

"Quiero una Corona," one said. "I got it down."

"That's all you need to know," another said.

"This is it; this is the place."

"You got that right, buddy."

Martha and I stopped to let them pass. Martha opened her mouth to speak, then cut herself off. She kissed me without prompting.

We walked past some new condos and down to the waterfront. Merchants' stalls stood loaded with silver jewelry and brightly painted wooden fish. Martha saw a satchel, made in Guatemala, and we bought it for her. Past the catamarans and the tourists' cruises of the bay that took you past Lovers' Beach out to Land's End, we came upon some stone jettys. There were no tourists. A few local families fished there. With them they had dogs and small children. Martha spoke with the kids and smiled at them. Kids always liked her.

"Martha, you're so good with kids," I said. I was being sincere.

"Stop it," she said.

"They love you."

"That's enough," she said.

We went out on the rocks and sat down.

The color of the light and the sea and the sky was gorgeous and we talked about it for a little while.I slipped my arm around Martha and she put her head on my chest.

She sat up quickly.A man was fishing from the rocks on the next jetty. He looked like the man who had taken her purse, she said.

"Look," she said. "Over there. It looks like him."

"It's not," I said.

"A strong resemblance," she said.

"You shouldn't have done it without telling me."

"We can't talk about that now. It was too long ago. It won't do any good."

I didn't argue this time. She was probably right. The sun was dropping quickly as it does near the end. When she sat back down, she stayed a few inches away from me. We were not touching at any place at all now.

"We didn't go sailing with that nice man I met last night," she said.

"No," I said.

"You didn't really want to," she said.

"Yes, I do. Let's set it up for tomorrow."

She looked through her new satchel, moving things around, shifting some items to the pockets of her shorts.

"I can't find his number. I was too drunk last night. I must have lost it."

"There it goes," I said. Only a sliver of the sun remained above the horizon.

"Things are happening so quickly. We don't have much time left here," she said.

"That's true," I said.

"It's night," she said.

The sun was gone.

"I'm hungry," I said. "How about you? Let's find a restaurant."

She didn't say anything, but she stood up.I took her elbow. The dusk was purple and pink. We walked along the rocks and back to town.

Part Two: Finisterra

The next day we take a taxi to the business district.

The money Martha has wired for has come.

In the middle of the street, several men surround us. They want us to buy something.

Martha buys a newspaper. But not from one of them.

"Compre el periodico," she says.

They follow us anyway.

It is the middle of a hot afternoon. A man is holding a beer. I offer to buy the beer for 1500 pesos. He gives the bottle to me. It is already open. The man did not want to sell it to me, but he sold it to me anyway. It is hot out, so I drink it. The man puts his money in his pocket, not a wallet.

The streets are unpaved. The curbstones are high. We walk in the street. Both of us are wearing sandals. A fine dust covers Martha's carefully painted toenails.

We eat lunch at a place away from the center of town, then return for a drink. Outside The Giggling Marlin the group of men is back. They seem glad to see us.

We have begun to feel the heat and the beer. Martha and the men are talking. I cannot understand them. She is smiling and gracious. She is rich and I am not. It was her idea to come here. I clean my fingernails with a penknife while they talk.

We shop for jewelry on the main streets. I buy a black coral necklace and earrings for Martha. She buys me a bolo tie with a chunk of black onyx set in silver.

The town is not crowded with tourists. The locals are all sleeping. It is midafternoon, over 100 degrees again, and we are once more walking around the marina. On one jetty, a family of six is fussing with a beat up old skiff. The kids are all small, dirty and nearly naked. They are laughing and playing with their dog. About a dozen pelicans are resting on a rock. Martha loves pelicans and asks me to take a picture. The kids come over and want me to take their pictures, too. They hold out their hands. My camera is not a Polaroid. I have nothing to give them.

Martha is laughing at me. She tells me again how beautiful the birds are. The family dog has noticed the pelicans. He rushes onto the rocks and barks. The birds do not move. He grabs one by a wing and starts to bite. Martha screams. I run onto the rocks and kick the dog. The dog growls, the kids scream. Their father looks at me like he knows. I start to hand him money, but instead I take Martha firmly by the hand and we walk briskly away.

I have not seen the men for hours. We eat dinner at a place we cannot find. We sit at a table on the sand. It is dark and there is no sign to tell us where we are. They serve shellfish and rice and corn and salsa. By now, we are quite drunk. We spend 150,000 pesos.

We are back in town at a place called the Corona Beach Club. The men are waiting outside. They smile and nod their heads as we enter.

Inside the strobe lights flash so often that I stop thinking. Martha rubs her long nails inside my shirt. I am covered with sweat. She puts her hands in my pockets and teases me. She smiles coyly. She starts to talk about the pelicans and the dog and she kids and me and herself, but the music starts again. It is so loud that I cannot hear her and she knows it but keeps on mouthing the words anyway. We drink three or four beers. I lose track. The whole while she is hugging me tightly, her whole arms around me.

Outside the men are still waiting. They offer us a ride back to our hotel.

Martha accepts. She tells them they are kind. In the hotel driveway, Martha invites them up to our room. They accept her invitation. Once inside, the men immediately lie down on the floor and fall asleep. Martha removes her clothes and climbs into bed on top of the sheets. The lights in the room are still on. She pulls me down on top of her. She is sure they're all asleep. I am nearly hallucinating from the heat and all the alcohol. She appears to be fine, though her smile seems a little odd now.

We have no plans to leave Mexico. We have given away our return tickets. It was Martha's idea. She was afraid that otherwise we had too little time.

In the morning, the men are still sleeping on the floor. Martha lays on the bed snoring, naked and uncovered. It is hot despite the air conditioner.

I stand up, cover Martha with a sheet, and pour myself some agua fresca from the refrigerator. The room is dark and loud because of the air conditioner. I think about turning it off, but instead I go out onto the balcony. It is fifteen degrees hotter outside. I drink down the water and go back inside for beer. I put several bottles of beer, Coronitas, in a bucket of ice and take the whole set-up outside. We are three stories up. The clouds seem close enough to touch. Like everything else they move slowly in the heat.

I think about the crowds of people in our lives—strangers, acquaintances, assorted hangers-on. Martha attracts them all. But there is no one close. What we once had, they are all gone. After a second beer, I pause to enjoy the view. From the balcony I can see the marina with its bustle and all the boats at the docks; I can see El Mar de Cortez and on the other side, the ocean and the end of the land.

Convenience

It was late at the 7-11 on Sunset and Normandie. The high and the low were grabbing for quick urges after the bars had closed; hot dogs, chips, sodas, frozen burritos. The young ones had all been to Florentine Gardens. Goth and grunge and punk all mixed up. Troy had been at Albert's house. Albert had a mixing board and dope.

Troy got a fake cappuccino by pushing a button. It tasted like bad hot chocolate. He asked the clerk if it had caffeine in it. The clerk said yes.

The cops were at the back of the store, milling around, checking out what looked good. Because they were at the back of the store and they were actually buying things—one cop had his wallet out—no one paid them much notice. If he had known cops were present, Troy would have been nervous. Just on general principle.

Troy'd had his lucky nickel—a buffalo nickel or an Indian head, depending on your viewpoint—for nearly five years. Drunk, stoned, pussy-whipped, he never lost it, always kept track of that nickel. He even had the management rip out a restaurant booth when the coin slipped between the cushions one morning at breakfast.

At the counter, he pulled out a wad of ones and some change to pay for the coffee. It came to "1-0-8." Troy fumbled with his change and his bills. He stepped aside and while he was stuffing his money back into his pocket, he noticed a March of Dimes collection box. It was chock full of money—mostly change, some bills. Troy wondered for a moment if the money really got to the disabled children. Maybe the clerk took it all out at the end of his shift and bought some serious smoke. Troy decided he was being cynical and selfish, so he pulled his money back out in order to deposit some coin at least in the box. He felt clumsy that he was taking so long. He should have been out the door by now. This redhead was staring at him disapprovingly. Troy didn't notice that the cops were next in line. Hurriedly, he dropped about a half-dozen coins into the slot.

"Shit," Troy shouted. He saw that—unintentionally, of course—he had shoved his lucky nickel into the box along with the quarters, dimes, nickels, and pennies he didn't care a whit about.

"Fuck! Fuck!! Fuck!!!" His voice got louder. Without thinking, he grabbed the entire March of Dimes box from the counter, took the top off and began frantically searching for his lucky charm. Unwittingly, and with nowhere else convenient to put it, he began dropping sorted coins, not back into the box, but into a backpack he was carrying and which he had set on the counter.

The clerk shouted, "Thief!!!" The cops, startled from their late night stupor, turned on their professional veneer. They grabbed Troy from behind. Cognizant only of his missing nickel, Troy swung his arms: "Get the fuck away from me, man. I gotta get my nickel."

The cops snapped his arms behind his back and cuffed him. "Robbery, resisting arrest, assaulting a police officer." They escorted Troy outside to their patrol car, reading him his rights and delineating the charges against him. They took the March of Dimes box as evidence. One cop counted the money as the other one drove. When they booked him, they filed the theft as grand larceny. Troy couldn't believe there was over two hundred dollars in that box. It made him feel good about society, about the world and his fellow human beings, to think that people would be so generous—even at a 7-11.

Gin and Juice

"I'm gonna get the fucker."

"Yeah, cool, man. Smoke his ass."

"That piece of shit!"

"Cool, man, where's the Sapphire?"

Marcus was looking for the bottle T put behind the couch. T couldn't remember shit. And I couldn't say shit.

"Light this up, man." T handed Marcus a spliff. Marcus pulled hard on the joint and passed it to T, then passed out a couple of blues he'd had in his pocket and washed it all down with the Bull.

T stayed in focus.

"Where's my fucking glock, shooter?"

"Where's the fucking gin?"

Marcus put on some porn.

"That's one big ass dick."

"You gay or some shit?"

"Fuu-uck..."

"How you looking at his dick when you got tits like that on the screen?"

T pointed to the television screen. His hand was shaking.

"They fake, man," Marcus said.

"How the fuck you know?"

"They don't fucking move, man. She's getting rammed hard up the ass and her fucking titties don't even bounce."

"So."

"So, she look like one of them TV reporters, their hair don't move in the wind and shit."

"Look at your fucking hair, shitbird. That shit went out of style—damn, fucking Nero knows when?"

"Nero?"

"Yeah, you ignorant fuck. The Roman fucking emperor."

"Just watch the fucking movie."

Our apartment had a TV and a couch. Nothing else.

I was sleeping most time during this whole debate. Silly ass shit. I had shit on my mind, man. T and Marcus wouldn't remember jack in the AM and they was no fucking good for what I wanted—up or down.

"We some sorry-ass motherfuckers, sitting here watching this shit and bickering like bitches. Let's throw a fucking party tomorrow night," I said.

"Cool," T said and passed out.

"Yeah," Marcus said. "Cool."

***

There was gin and juice in the fridge—nice and cold. The kind in a can, but beggars can't be choosers. Commendations to the Gem who put it there. No one else did shit. Me included.

Every one was late so I was alone for about an hour. Marcus and T were out somewhere. Supposed to be getting shit for the party, but I think they was getting some blow.

Ark was the first to show. A good sign and a bad. I didn't want him fucked up. I wanted to talk.

I had some acid jazz on low, but Ark liked loud.

"Hey, man, where's the thump?"

"What you want?"

"Put some Biggie on the box, man."

I stuck on "Life After Death" and he started to move.

I had an agenda with Ark, but later.

Next came Sessa—alone—and we had to go dead in the tracks.

Top: low cut. Bottom: high cut. Tits, legs, tight in the ass.

Snow came next and then Paulie, and Lisa, and Tomcat, and pretty soon it was a full house.

And, as much as I've always and forever wanted to fuck Sessa, she wasn't what I was interested in. Not at all.

***

Well, shit. The Gem sucked me long and hard in the bathroom, so I missed my shot with Ark and Paulie, which was the whole fucking reason for goin' thru all this shit. After I'd come in her mouth, and ate her out real good, and sucked her toes, one-by-one, real good, then I unlocked the bathroom door—Lord knows how long we'd been inside. All these fuckers outside the head had been screaming and I'd told them to fuck off and piss out a window and then forgot about them. Shit, some of them had pissed out the fucking window and any other motherfuckin' place, and they were so hopped up and wanted to fuck me up so bad, so I told them the Gem was sick and I was getting her well; they all liked the Gem, so they believed me, or something like that, so I got off Scott-free, a smile—no, a shit-eating grin —on my face. Anyway, when we got done and got out, Ark and Paulie was so fucked up, we couldn't talk about shit—let alone something so paused as what I wanted to discuss.

I'll give you an example of where things were at:

"Do gay bars have to have two bathrooms?"

"Huh? What the fuck are you talking about?"

"By law, I mean..."

"What the fuck you talking about?"

"Like there ain't no bitches there, so why have a ladies' room?"

"Shee-it."

***

I lost the entire next day because we was so hung over.

***

"Hey, Laze, what you say?"

I thought we could knock over the Hancock. The Gem had walked out, which made me strong sad. I needed her support. But she said 'no bad shit; nothing vee the law.

Ark and Paulie wanted more Jack. No more, no less. No deal.

Finally, "Fuck you," I said. "You ain't worth a shit, you know that?"

All of them, more than just Ark and Paulie was so fucked up, and remained so, that I walked out all the way, the whole shot.

"I'll do it by my fucking self," I said.

***

I got the fuck out for four days, no intention of doing shit, of course. Not a goddamn fucking thing. Let them think whatever the fuck they wanted, the shit-ass, no-ambition-motherfuckers.

If I ain't shit, at least I ain't shinola. I ain't shit after the shower, and I ain't shoveling shit against the tide. Fuck 'em if they can't take a joke. I'd show the motherfuckers, I would.

I had to get some cash or I couldn't convince a dead rat of what I was going to say: 'I knocked the 'Cock and got four hundred bucks.' I ripped the only phone book in town out of a booth near PJ's and started calling for work. Manpower, Apple Temporaries, Kelly Services...That's right. My mother worked there. That's where I heard it. I'd be a fucking Kelly Girl. Yeah! Make the bucks. Get props. And then some: maybe a little Sessa on the side.

It was shit work, man. Washing floors, scrubbing toilets, cleaning all these fucking fancy offices after dark. No one else around, not a soul. But shitloads of us; all over the place. Couldn't tell the supervisors apart from us. Same look. All of us cleaning—them watching, too. Lots of shit I wanted to stick in my pockets. Expensive stuff on desk tops: good pens, silver picture frames, crystal shit. Like Bugsy had at the Flamingo. Just tons of stuff. But I told myself: Keep your fucking eyes on the prize. More than anything I needed four hundred bucks. Bad.

.

***

Incommunicado: four days.

***

Back on the corner: "Real easy shit, man. Nothing to it."

"How much you get?"

"Four bills."

"Bullshit."

I flashed the cash.

"You hit the Hancock? How the fuck you gonna buy from there now, man? You supposed to rob shit away from home—like don't shit where you eat, my friend."

"He didn't see my ass. My disguise was the fucking bomb and I did voices and shit."

Ark said, "What the fuck you mean, 'voices?'"

"Like an accent and shit."

"Let's hear that shit," Paulie said.

I did 'Give me all your money' in a redneck accent like I heard in Deliverance. I raised my voice a notch or two, high almost like a girl or Ross Fucking Perot.

The whole crew cracked up, Sessa, too—standing now at the back of the circle crowded around me, but edging forward.

Then T said, "Shit, you guys all acting like you disbelieve him and shit, but, fuck, he got four C's in his mothefuckin' pocket and you ain't got shit. From where I'm sitting, shit, he the fucking man."

I could see Sessa smiling at the back. But I was just bullshitting myself. I wan't goin' to mac on the Gem, with her at work and all, and a smile from Sessa hardly put me between her sheets. Shit, Ice Cube used that riff from the Isleys in a song about not using no AK. Romantic, shit.

But T was bouncing. "I'm goin' to get me some fucking cash. If it's that fucking easy, the motherfucker deserves to lose his fuckin' money. No offense, Blueberry, but you ain't no hard core, man."

"I wouldn't, man," I said.

"Fuck, he always treat me like dogshit anyway, every time I go in there to buy something, he watching me all the time and shit. Can't even get to the fucking Fritos, he almost falling over the counter trying to eyeball me and I ain't ever stolen shit from his fuckin' ass."

T was all wound up. What the fuck could I do?

"Hey, Blueberry, how much you get again, four hundred?"

"Yeah, but don't try it, man. I know he's beefing up security. Gettin'a gun, maybe a guard, I don't know. He's had some shoplifting and shit in there, too, you know."

"Oh, fuck that. What you doin'? You want all the goods for your own ass or something?"

"No, T. Shit, man, I was goin' to share around anyway. Throw a big fuckin' party for all of us and shit. I don't need this kind of bucks for me."

"I do," T said. And he just blew.

Nothing else I could do. Not even tell the truth; I mean, before maybe —but now T was gone. I checked his house, I checked PJ's—Richie was bartending; said he didn't see him all night. I went to Food 4 Less. Gem had already gotten off work. Two hours ago.

I went to the Hancock; bought a fifth of Jack. All quiet, no action.

Gem found me drunk, passed out at the pad.

The next day we heard the news: T was dead, blasted in the face with a shotgun fired by the owner, who kept it within easy reach, just behind the counter and right by the cash register. The following day, we read it in the Papers: Local Store Owner Prevents Armed Robbery; New Neighborhood Hero Beats Back Crime.

I gave the four C notes to the Gem.

Indignity

Mark got Ronnie to strip for him. Ron De Jean put on his mother's clothes and took them off to the sound of her Big Band records. She was a stripper, so she had all the right wardrobe. Mark made him use everything —the spike heels, the padded bras, the lace g-strings, the garter belts, the feather boas. There were about ten of us, drinking beer and crammed into Ronnie's living room and we were howling. Ron was small and girlish and he pulled off his role well. He even seemed to be enjoying himself, after nearly crying when Mark had to threaten him to make him do it. He was so good that Manny even flirted with the idea of going home to get his trumpet to play along, but we were already loud enough.

After an especially raunchy number, where Ronnie shook and rattled the curves of his soft ass to the sounds of that old blues tune about "squeezing my lemon until the juice flows down my leg," sung by I'm-not-sure-who, maybe Koko Taylor, with some muted trumpets and trombones in back of her—not that heavy-sounding Led Zeppelin version—after that song, with Ronnie all smiles and proud of himself, and the rest of us holding our bellies from laughing so much, Mark unzipped his fly, took out his big cock, and it was hard.

"Ronnie, get over here and suck me off," Mark said.

Ronnie went over and made a few fake bobbing motions something like air guitar, but Mark was serious. He grabbed Ronnie by the hair and pushed him down onto his cock.

"Do it!" he said.

Ronnie had no choice; he got down on his knees in front of Mark, who was seated in a big armchair, old and torn, but once-fine furniture. Red crushed velvet. Mark slouched down and his head lolled back as Ronnie started working hard. Ronnie gagged and Mark slapped him.

"Take the whole fucking thing, you faggot," he said.

After the slap, Mark came quickly. He thrust his cum hard, in waves and spasms, into Ronnie's mouth.

He said now, with both roughness and affection, "Don't you dare spit that out. You swallow that shit now; it's fucking good. It's nutritious, man." Then he patted Ronnie's head.

Meanwhile, Bobby and Richie had taken their dicks out; they were hard, too, and they were jerking off.

"Hey, hey, Richie, what the fuck you doing? Why you doing yourself when we got Little Miss Showgirl to do it for you?" Mark asked. "Hey, Ronnie, get over there and suck Richie off."

Ronnie hesitated.

"What the fuck you waiting for?" Mark asked.

"No, Mark, it's OK. Really." Richie stammered and tried to stick it back in his pants.

"He's good, Rich, real good. Ain't you, Ronnie?"

"Mark, he's a guy."

"He did me," Mark said. "Are you calling me a faggot?"

"Ah, no...I didn't say that. Shit no."

"Ronnie, get your ass over there and give Richie a good blow job. Then do Bobby."

Ronnie stopped crying and did Richie and Bobby, and then, without further prompting, he did Tony and Jim, interspersing a dance or two between the action. We kept the music flowing and we decimated his mother's liquor cabinet. We drank and talked and tried to be comfortable while the blow jobs went on, but there really wasn't much time to waste. No one lasted more than a couple of minutes. Ronnie was actually quite good at it, and we were quite young.

Jim was the quickest to come, and when it was over, Ronnie announced, "Hey, I think my mother's going to be home soon."

Mark said, "Do one more. You gotta do one more. You gotta do Tom."

Ronnie said, "She'll be home any minute. I gotta clean up. You guys gotta go."

"Fucking blow Tom, I said." Mark started towards Ronnie.

Ronnie dropped down on his knees in front of me and started fiddling with my fly.

Now I admit I had been hard the whole time. But I wasn't going to do shit with Ronnie, and, not in front of these guys.

"Let's do the real thing," I heard myself saying.

"What's the matter, Tom? You better than the rest of us?" Jim asked.

"You ain't a fag unless you take it up the ass. Ain't that right, Ronnie?"

"What do you mean, the 'real thing?'" Tony asked.

I had on Levi 501s with the button fly instead of a zipper, so Ronnie was taking a long time with my pants, but he could tell I was hard.

"Mrs. Ronnie's a stripper...." I said.

"She ain't gonna fuck us, asshole," Mark said. "We're kids."

Ronnie froze in front of me. I wouldn't look at him. I didn't want to see his face.

"We can pay her..."

Ronnie stood up. "My mother's a dancer, not a whore."

"Shut the fuck up," Rich said. This time he slapped Ronnie. "I want some real pussy, and your mother's fine...."

"I don't think it's a good idea," Mark said. "Let's get the fuck out of here.

Tom'll get the first blow job next time."

"Yeah, let's split," I said quickly.

"Wait a fucking minute," Tony said. "Next time? What's this next time shit, Mark. This ain't Glitter Gulch and Ronnie's a little faggot, I don't care what you say..."

"I am not a fag..."

"Shut the fuck up, Ronnie, I'm talking," Tony continued. "And, I don't really give a shit. You ain't Nina Hartley either."

Tony turned to the rest of us. We were bunched up in the middle of the living room like a football team in a huddle, near the door but not quite. Tony spread his arms out like he was giving a speech on the floor of Congress. "But Mrs. Fucking Ronnie, now there's some real opportunity. Single mother of the year...What would you say, maybe 38 years old, tops. Dances five nights a week or some shit, so she's in great shape. Tits like Pamela Lee...Tom, what you have in mind, what's it worth to you? Come on, guys, what do you say? Ten bucks apiece? Fifteen? We can offer her some real money..."

"I'm with Mark. I say we leave," I said.

"Fuck that, Tom, it was your fucking idea," Jim said.

Tony collected the money. Eight guys, ten bucks each. Eighty dollars. Mark wouldn't kick in. Tony let him slide. He had to. I was last to pony up. Tony pushed me hard. I gave in and kicked in twenty. I had to. That made a hundred.

Tony was fanning the bills—there were singles in the wad so it didn't look too classy—when we heard the keys in the door.

"Oh, shit. Oh, shit...." Ronnie was in tears again. He ran into his room. I had to do the talking. I couldn't get out of it.

Mrs. De Jean walked in wearing leather pants and heels. Tits up high. Red toenails, red fingernails. She really did look great.

"What the hell's going on here?" she asked.

"Oh, hi, Mrs. De Jean," I said. I was doing a good job sounding nonchalant. "We were just hanging out with Ronnie tonight. He's a really great guy."

"Well, I'm glad you think so, but you gotta go now. I just got back from work and I'm beat."

She said nothing about the beer cans and empty whiskey bottles all over her apartment. She looked truly tired.

"I'll bet it's hard work," Tony said from the back.

"Don't get smart with me. It's bedtime, boys..."

"Well, you know, funny you should put it that way," I interrupted. "Because we have a proposition for you." I showed her the money. I could see Ronnie peeking out of his bedroom. He never crossed the threshold and he never said shit.

"I hope you're not thinking what I think you're thinking," she said. She put a cigarette to her lips. I lit it for her. "Because I don't fuck for money, and

I don't fuck teenagers period for any reason. It's time to go."

"Come on, Mrs. D. Be a sport." Jim threw in his two cents. I couldn't really see Mark. He seemed to be crouching in the middle. Forget about him, I thought.

"I'm flattered, guys. But save your money and save your breath. It's beddie-bye time."

She looked irresistible dragging on that smoke. A Lucky Strike. I had wanted out so bad, but now I needed to give it one more try.

"We ain't cheapskates, Mrs. D. This is a hundred bucks," I said, fanning the bills like a Vegas high roller.

"Your generosity overwhelms me," she quipped, then got serious, even tender. She was looking right at me, softly. "I'm sorry. I know you're sincere and I'm not going to preach to you about exotic dancing...I love what I do, but I don't do this. We gotta say goodnight."

All of a sudden, Mark lunged out from the group. He tackled Mrs. D around her knees.

"Fuck you, then, bitch. We won't pay you shit. But we're getting us some pussy." He was all over her in a second. He was strong as Draino. He ripped at her hair, tore off her clothes, shredding the shit out of them. Mrs. D screamed and Mark slapped her. Then he covered her mouth with his big hand. Ronnie came out and tried to jump Mark from behind, but he just turned and backhanded the kid, close-fisted, right in the jaw, and Ronnie fell to the floor, bleeding. None of the rest of us moved an inch.

I don't know what happened next, but by the end of the night, we'd all been at her. A couple of us twice. I'd like to blame Mark, of course, but that would be bullshit. He took a long time, and he didn't even come. The rest of the time, he just watched us. Mrs. D was brutalized, but she managed a joke at Mark's expense amidst her tears, and he didn't even hit her.

After about an hour, maybe an hour and a half, when it was over, Ronnie emerged. His jaw was clearly broken. Mark was indeed that strong. With all that happened, however, Ronnie wasn't crying any more. Neither was Mrs. D. Ronnie comforted his mother and cleaned her up. She did the same for him, washing the blood from his face with a paper towel. They hugged and held each other in the complete and awful silence of their apartment at 3 AM.

"Let's go," Mark said, and we all followed him out without a word.

Mrs. D never called the cops, never told a soul what had happened. For a week or so, none of us did either. Then the bragging started. By the end of the next week, the story was that she'd come home and offered to do us all for free, that she had fifty orgasms and we each had three, that she had coke and hash and that we tooted and smoked until dawn.

This all happened in July. By September, Ronnie and his mother were gone. We heard they had moved to Canada, but of course, we never knew for sure. We never heard a word from them or about them again.

Josie at the Blue Light

When we met every day at the Blue Light Tavern we were all out of work. Danny was out on strike. Paul had never worked. And I had just been laid off.

She came in dressed in some kind of an Aztec outfit. She said her name was Josefina.

We took bets on who could score her.

Over a pool game that night Paul hit Danny with a cue stick. The whole place broke out in a fight. I got my nose busted for about the eighth time. Josie took care of me.

"I like your mustache," she said.

I took her home and I didn't stay. She kissed me at the door when I left. It was a long kiss, and tempting.

I had a box of dog bones in the back of the car. I ran out to get them. I gave them to her for Sammy, her boxer. (My dog had run away the year before.) Then I said goodnight.

Back at the Blue Light they had a crew cleaning up. It was just the regular guys. The bar's owner, Charlie H., had offered them a case of beer to do the work. I pitched in. It felt like a job.

The Blue Light had pool tables, three of them, and backless chairs. It was a windowless place, but the door was always open. In the day time, light shot through like a bright beam right in front of the bar, sketching sights to see. In the sunlight you could watch the drops of moisture on the shiny bar top glisten like quartz, the cigarette smoke rise in a halo above the patrons' heads, and the dust particles descend down on your drink like invaders from space. Take your pick. One time I tried to close the door because the sun was in my eyes, but Charlie came out from behind the bar right away and opened it again. He didn't say anything about it and neither did I.

Now it was 3 AM. I swept glass from the linoleum floor, shook my head at the shattered pinball game, my favorite, and drank three more Michelobs. Charlie and I got to talking and he said he thought Josie was weird. He said he knew her from before. I got sore and left.

At home I poured some Jack Daniels, threw away some bills that had come in the mail, and jacked off about Josie's big ass.

I have these mini-blinds in my apartment—I got them from Sears at a sale—but the sun comes right through, so I woke up early the next morning even though I had no reason to. It was summer and there were already kids playing punch ball in the street.

I had no cigarettes and I was facing a long walk to the store because Alfie's on the corner had closed after 75 years as a family business. When he was open, every one bitched about Alfie and his son because of their high prices. Now that he's gone we are all sad.

The 7-11 is up on the boulevard, about a mile away. Inside, a young black girl at the cash register was admiring her own fingernails, which were about three inches long and fake. When I paid I told her they were nice. She had some pictures airbrushed on them and I spent a few minutes looking them over. The store was not busy. She seemed very happy that I liked them.

Outside I broke up a fight among thirteen year olds. Two of them were trying to take the other kid's bike. I sent the kid on the bike on his way and held the thieves by the collar until he was long gone. Then I let them go.

The girl with the nails came outside to thank me. She told me that her uncle owned the franchise and she could get me a job. I guess I had mentioned that I wasn't working. I agreed to meet with the guy the next day. We set up an interview for two o'clock.

She said that her name was Natasha and that she was glad to meet me.

***

That night Josie was back at the Blue Light. She was dressed altogether different. She had on a gold bikini top and a short leather mini skirt. Her stomach bulged some below her tits but it looked sort of nice on her. She hung all over me and I was thrilled.

I bought her drinks. She drank Cuba Libres and I had Coronas and an occasional shot of bourbon. Josie had a lot of quarters in her purse and we put them all in the juke box. At first we danced fast and the guys teased us. Josie hiked her skirt up and mooned them. She wasn't wearing underwear. Around one we were pretty drunk. She put five dollars worth of quarters in the box—all on slow songs. By the time Lionel Ritchie came on, singing "Three Times a Lady," I had my hand under her skirt.

I took her home again and this time she was ready. She had sangria and tequila and limes all laid out on her kitchen table. We slow-danced again and again and our clothes fell off slowly, too. Josie had bleached her hair blonde but her skin was olive and Latin and smooth. She had probably forty pounds on her but I loved it—the tits, the ass, the powerful thighs.

At dawn she pushed me to the ground and sat on my face. She ground her clit on my lips and tongue and slapped my face.

"Come mi coño," she said, at first softly; then she shouted: "Come mi coño. Lick me. Lick me, you asshole."

She came quickly, then wanted it again. She had fifteen or twenty orgasms grinding on my face. We knocked over lamps and end tables, and finally, a book case. While she rested I looked at the titles. The were mostly in Spanish, some in French; I could not read them, though I thought a couple were dirty.

She was covered with sweat. The smell was powerful and sexy. My face hurt. She rose up off me and grabbed my cock firmly. She stroked it quickly and with pressure, digging in her ragged, sharp nails from time to time. Her nails caught my flesh and a small trickle of blood flowed down my shaft. I was hard as a rock.

She climbed on and rode hard. I tried to hold back but I ejaculated quickly. Josie reassured me. She climbed on again, rocking me a little less hard. When I came again she held me close and whispered, "Yo te amo. Yo te amo."

We slept through the next day and started all over at night. We never left her apartment except to go to the liquor store. We sent for pizza and Chinese food at meal times.

The third night I woke up in the dark with a start. I felt something cold against my throat. Josie was looming over me with a switchblade against my neck.

"I'm going to kill you, Juan," she said. "You're going to pay."

She said this several times.

Juan isn't my name, of course.

"What are you doing?" I shouted. "I'm Bobby. We met at the Blue Light."

She was sitting on my chest and her forty extra pounds came in handy.

"Fuck you, Juan," she said. "You're gonna die."

We struggled over the knife. She was quite strong. Eventually I got it out of her hand. I came away with cuts on my face and hands.

The walls in the rooms of Josie's apartment were all painted yellow. I kissed her while she slept before I walked out the door.

***

The next day I walked up to the 7-11. The girl with the nails was there behind the counter, together with an older guy who was very big and who I guessed was the uncle she had been talking about.

"Hi," I said.

She did not answer.

"New color." I nodded at her nails. "I like it."

"You let me down," she said.

"I was..." I started to explain.

"I know what you were doing," she said. "I know everything."

I tried to sound like I didn't believe her, but somehow I did. Natasha ignored me while she waited on a brief rush of customers. I stared at the signs on the walls and on the windows: BIG GULP 69 cents, DIET PEPSI $1.99 six pack, LOTTO PLAY AND WIN, et cetera. One of her customers had green hair.

"You could have had me and a job," she said once she had a break.

I had only talked to her for five minutes four nights ago, but I believed her on this one, too.

"You'd better go," she said. "My uncle's here today and he's big."

I shrugged.

"I mean it," she said. "Don't come around here any more."

"I really don't understand," I said, lying through my teeth. The cuts on my face and hands hurt like hell. I tried to smile, but I knew she wasn't kidding. I walked out the door like she asked and headed straight for the Blue Light.

Trying to Get AIDS

She had long blonde hair.

"I have the AIDS virus," she said.

"Yes," I said.

She had "HIV+" tattooed on one of her large breasts.

"I hate condoms," she said.

"Yes."

"I only do men who are positive."

"I understand." I lied—by implication at least. I'd never even had a single STD.

Everything about her was long—she was tall; she had an aquiline nose, long fingernails and long toenails—unpolished, but filed to a point.

She cleared her throat.

I handed her the envelope with the money in it.

"It's freeing in a way, isn't it?" she said as she got me hard with her hand and her fingernails.

"Yes."

"You're shy?"

"Most of the time," I said. I was sweating around my hairline and on my upper lip. I could hear the pulsing at my temples.

I was slumped on the couch, my pants off and my legs open wide. I stretched my neck, rolling my head around, trying to relax. Her apartment was very clean—fresh white walls, no marks, no dust, nice paintings and photos, fresh flowers, healthy green plants.

She clenched my cock tight in her nails as she stroked me.

"I like to draw blood," she said.

"That's fine. I like it, too."

She moved her hand firmly, but slowly—just perfect.

She changed positions. She laid back on the floor and put her feet up on my cock and balls and dug in with her toenails. She kneaded my dick between her arches. I could feel my shaft wet with my own blood. It stung nicely. I was very hard. I thought I might come too quickly. But I let go and I lost my thoughts entirely—just like I wanted to.

She pulled her pants off and straddled me on the couch. Her ribs and her pelvic bones jutted through the skin of her vein-thin frame. Her menses were running down her legs.

"Eat me," she said.

She thrust against my face and I licked her and tongued her and made her come. She tasted like metal. Her orgasm was big, and she shook strongly and screamed. She collapsed, nearly in tears, onto my lap, and she took full, deep breaths. She put her arms tightly around my neck and she dug her nails into my shoulders.

When she was through, she got up and thrust down onto my cock, wrapping her dripping cunt around it, hard still and bleeding now from the cuts made by her fingernails and her toenails. She fucked me hard, jumping up and down on my shaft, her pelvic bone crashing down on my balls. I loved it. I was really lost in it now. I could think of nothing but the ecstasy of the fuck; I'd never had better, so thrilling, so wild, so out there, the best I'd ever had. When I shot my cum inside her, it all came back to me: I never really take risks; I'd turned down so many thrills in my life. I'd never thought seriously of suicide before, never imagined—in any detail—my own death. But I could see it now and I felt calm and purposeful. The headache I'd had, seemingly for years, was gone and my mind felt clear.

I never keep thrusting after I come; with her, I did. I couldn't stop. I paid more money. I stayed the night. We did it over and over. I'd recommend her to anyone.